AMERICAN

ATLAS

AMERICAN

ATLAS

A NOVEL

DAN GERBER

PRENTICE-HALL, INC.
Englewood Cliffs, N.J.

American Atlas by Dan Gerber
Copyright © 1973 by Dan Gerber
All rights reserved. No part of this book may be
reproduced in any form or by any means, except
for the inclusion of brief quotations in a review,
without permission in writing from the publisher.
Printed in the United States of America
Prentice-Hall International, Inc., London
Prentice-Hall of Australia, Pty. Ltd., North Sydney
Prentice-Hall of Canada, Ltd., Toronto
Prentice-Hall of India Private Ltd., New Delhi
Prentice-Hall of Japan, Inc., Tokyo

---

10 9 8 7 6 5 4 3 2 1

Library of Congress Cataloging in Publication Data

Gerber, Daniel F
  American atlas.

  I. Title.
PZ4.G3615.Am [PS3557.E66]   813'.5'4   73–62
ISBN 0–13–023879–1

The poem, "Sources," appeared originally in *The Ohio Review.*

For
Sam Furda
and everyone who ever hung out at his gas station
and
of course
Clyde Henson

You are in the West, but free to live in your East, as ancient as you need—and to live well there.

—Rimbaud

. . . the girl in the red sweater painting watercolors by a lake in Michigan who waved at him with her brushes, not to say farewell but out of hope, because she did not know that she was watching a train with no return passing by.

—Gabriel Garcia Márquez

PART 1

1

When my father died my shoes began to pinch, and my shirt felt as if it would rip across the back. I turned my head quickly, but there was no one looking over my shoulder. I stood before a mirror but couldn't mimic the faces I had made so often. My jaw seemed broader and my eyes deeper set. I was no longer a son.

I have never wanted to look at the dead, and in fact I detest the word. It falls like a lump, like the weight of something unpleasant you've carried a long way without stopping; past, forgotten, void, without the life of "dying" or the sonorous quality of "death." *Sane and sacred death* —the previews I'd had in a bottle of codeine, the world closed up in another room and the blankets pressing down on me, or when I was lying on the pavement, when I'd broken every bone I owned, the blood running from my eyes and ears, I thought, Oh, you're going to die. That's too bad, what a silly way for it to happen. And I knew I should have been sorry to see Gloria waving good-bye and growing small.

My father's body seemed large to me, as if it had swollen to epic proportions, like the statues of Lenin I'd seen in *The National Geographic,* and I looked down at him from a great height. I turned and walked out in the middle of the service, only vaguely aware of the glaring faces of my relatives. I started the car, shoved in the tape of Janis Joplin singing "Get It While You Can," and headed out of town, lost in the music and feeling stronger than the car in my hands, owning the country that passed by me.

There's no point in pretending my actions were forgivable, that I could have or would have wanted to go back, to apologize, to slink around like a wet dog, pretending I hadn't known what I was doing. I knew exactly what I was doing, and I think my father might have understood, though that no longer mattered.

It was exhilarating to feel the dry pavement whirring softly under my tires, thinking of all that dark maroon mourning I'd escaped, that choking, tear-soaked ritualized world. I felt I was being fired from a cannon of murk, not sure where I was going but knowing I'd be able at least to breathe there. I dropped the Porsche into fifth gear and cruised at an indicated one hundred miles an hour. The Porsche was a concession, a tolerated deviation from the prescribed image for "a young man who would someday run this company." I remember Martin O'Donnell, the company comptroller, taking it upon himself to set me straight. He called me into his office one afternoon to talk about "things your father might not tell you."

"You know you have quite a responsibility around here," he began. "People are looking at you and wondering if you'll fill the bill." His glasses slid down his nose, and he dipped his head and peered at me over the rims like Barry Fitzgerald. "There was some speculation as to whether your father'd be able to fill your grandfather's shoes, and I remember a lot of people had their doubts. Well, he did, and that's history, but he was also very conscientious about the kind of example he set for the employees, and that's what I want to talk to you about."

"Oh."

He tugged at his vest and continued.

"You see, people are watching you, not so much what you actually do, as your deportment."

"Oh."

"Yes, the way you dress, the hours you keep, the way you conduct your life in the community. That coat you're wearing, for example; this isn't a country club. Your father would never wear a sport coat to the office, and those loafers aren't a businessman's shoes."

I felt blood gorging my brain.

"It's important that you're here early and that you're one of the last people to leave after five. And don't put your feet on your desk. I saw you with your feet on the desk the other day, and I almost couldn't believe it. The people around here don't really know what kind of a job you're doing, but they do know when you put your feet on your desk, and it creates a lax attitude all around you."

"You mean it's not what I do, but how I look?"

"Well, frankly, that's the core of it. You don't have to be awfully smart, but it's awfully important that you be very businesslike."

I could see myself in slow motion, tipping over the desk, ripping into the filing cabinets with a crowbar and scattering figures all over his businesslike office, smashing a Bancroft Custard Cream Pie, the big twenty-four-ounce family size, into his CPA face, smearing his blue serge lapels with frozen whipped cream.

After a long drive I returned at night and broke into my own house. Well, not really broke in; I used my key, though the fact that I'd parked my car at the end of the long driveway and tiptoed into the house with a flashlight, brought the fast pulse of all my imagined crimes. I ripped one check from the checkbook in the kitchen drawer, wrote "Thanks" on the stub, and stuffed the check into my shirt pocket, along with my passport. When I put the book back into the drawer, I discovered a tube of lipstick. Gloria handed me her lipstick every time we went out. Each lipstick commemorated a boring party or a colon-twisting evening with the family, when I either had to drink a lot or suffer the stomach cramps and the blood-stuffed head that came from keeping my ears open and my mouth shut. When I did open my mouth it was worse.

It was November, the eve of elections. I don't even remember how the discussion turned to the war, but my sister was telling me how ashamed she was of my "anti-war activities," my letters to the editor of the Brainard *Republican*. My head began to contract. "You've been almost criminally irresponsible," she said. "How can you attack your country at a time of her great need? I'm embarrassed to try and explain it to my friends."

My mouth opened. "Don't talk to me about irresponsible. How could anyone be irresponsible to a country that welshes on all its Geneva agreements, butt-fucks Asia with an electric cattle prod, and shoots its own students because they're morally outraged?"

"If you're talking about those creeps at Kent State, they got just what they deserved."

"You don't mean that."

"Yes, I do."

"No, you don't. You're not thinking."

"I wish they'd shoot some more, then maybe they'd stop and think about what they're doing to their country."

"You goddamned stupid fascist cunt." The lid was off.

My brother-in-law rose to the defense. "You can't talk to my wife that way, you pinko bastard."

I was looking down at him from the center of the table. My shoes were splaying crystal and candlesticks. My hand was reaching for his collar. He was going to get the full rage I wanted to pour on my sister. "If you don't shut up, I'm going to knock your fucking teeth out." My voice sounded only vaguely familiar. My father buried his face in his hands. My sister clutched her breast and gasped, "Oh my God, oh my God." My brother-in-law fell over backward in his chair, my mother charged from her end of the table and began slapping me like a Chippewa Indian flailing wild rice, then ran from the room shrieking and crying. A steamy silence, and one last crystal goblet rolled off the table and splattered on the floor.

I took the lipstick from the drawer, pulled off the cap, applied the tip to the formica counter top, and in my very best penmanship wrote:

Gloria,

> The pupa has emerged.
> I think
> I love you
> I think

> Larry

2

There was an oasis at Ben Flatt's gas station where I'd worked Saturdays and summers when I was in high school. When I stopped to talk to Ben I was always eighteen, the football hero and surreptitiously admired Billy Badass, the hometown wild one who'd been sent off to what everyone suspected, with some justification, was a reform school in Arizona and returned with, they suspected, worldly knowledge that made parents apprehensive and intrigued their daughters. Ben had been a professional fighter who'd won a few preliminary bouts but had never been a contender. He had one defect for which no amount of training could compensate, short arms. He'd known the best of the light heavyweights, but his glory resided in the fact that he'd once sparred with Rocky Marciano.

Sometimes when I stopped at Ben's, we'd spar a few rounds in the back room with open hands, always pulling our punches, and talk about "how much water has gone over the dam" since the Brainard Wildcats had their undefeated season in '58, about what had happened to Charlie and Dink and Lamarza, how nobody saw anybody anymore, and about the night of the Farratville game when the temperature had dropped to ten degrees and Ben went down to the station and brought back cotton work gloves for all the linemen and defensive backs.

Ben would hold up his hand and I'd try to hit it, but no matter how I faked and jabbed, it was always an inch to the right or left of my fist. When I was in high school, Ben had broken my nose. I feinted and dodged and dropped my guard and ran into his knuckles. Ben was mortified but later told me I'd have to stop being such a fancy Dan, that I made it too hard for him to miss me. It irritated a lot of people that I continued to hang out at Ben's station, a lot of people like Martin O'Donnell.

I filled the Porsche and headed south. In the lower peninsula of Michigan, that's the only direction you can maintain on land. It is, after all, a peninsula. Travel has always brought stability to my life. When I'm at a dead end, when the shit is too thick to penetrate, the viatic freedom of scenery passing clears the air, takes me, at least momentarily, beyond the fact that the trouble with the world is that it's right now. If I was to avoid knocking the hat off every man I passed in the street and joining random funeral processions, I needed an almost total and continuous change of props. A destination seemed unimportant. Besides there was nowhere to go, never a place that was more than a point of departure. The important thing was to move, to keep the windows open and the scenery fresh.

I checked into a Howard Johnson Motel on the north side of Detroit about 2:00 A.M., scanned the TV for anything more engaging than a Johnny Weismuller Tarzan movie and took a brief inventory; one navy-blue dacron-and-wool mourner's uniform, one Burberry trench coat, my blank check, my American Express Card, my passport, and several assorted charge plates. I'd just put a check from my grandfather's trust in the bank, and my only messages home would be my bills and charge slips.

In the morning I felt dazed; a certain shivering in the bowels told me I might have gone too far. After copious suspicious looks, miniconferences and six pieces of identification, including my private pilot's license, my Abercrombie & Fitch charge plate, and an Honorary Sheriff's Deputy card, which I'd acquired bribing a real deputy on a reckless driving charge, and a short and uncomfortably informal chat with the branch vice-president, I exchanged the check for $5,000.00 in hundred-dollar bills at my bank's Detroit branch.

I walked out the glass doors and down the street without benefit of a Brink's escort or a concealed .38. The large inner pockets of the coat finally justified, my grub stake and petty cash kitty to a new life, a new theme song, and a new script in which the word "why" would not be allowed to exist. Heading back to my car, it occurred to me that I might even find use for the "D" rings on my coat, which in World War I would have dripped with grenades.

At Abercrombie's I bought a double shoulder holster money belt to fit under my shirt, a Safari Cloth bush jacket, a leather sport coat, pullovers, shirts, socks, underwear, slacks, two nylon suitcases, a folding Buck knife with a walnut handle and brass studs, a down-filled sleeping bag, a first-aid kit, a navy-blue nylon ski jacket, and a pair of Russell walking shoes. If there's one thing I believe in, it's equipment. I wasn't sure how I'd use it, but the time would come. I bought flare-bottom Levi's at a boutique down the street and a wide leather belt with a large buckle that resembled a brass monkey after the

Chicago fire, a razor and toothbrush from the corner drug, and a pair of mirror-finish Polaroid sunglasses.

I got on I–94 and headed straight west across the wrist of Michigan, the smoke, bowling, and organ music of Detroit growing smaller in my rear-view mirrors, a million miserable arc welders, die-cutters, purchasing agents, manufacturer's reps, whores, pimps, junkies, Lion fans, jockstrap sniffers, chrome, country clubs, ghettos, fire escapes, relish bars, love affairs, spoiled children, sales quotas, brand shares, pseudo-English subdivisions, beehive hairdos, gold-cup races, and the genuine imitation silk suit syndrome. Gloria had come from Detroit, and I'd been there three times, once to get married. I thought of Gloria reading my sign, glad I wasn't there. She'd cry and I'd say, "Gee, honey" (at thirty-one I still said "Gee," another reason for a new life). I'd say "Gee, honey, I'm sorry. I don't know why I act this way." Then I'd hug her, soak up a few tears in my shirt; we'd make love, she'd have an ostentatious orgasm and in the same breath ask me if I'd remembered to lock the garage. But I wasn't there, and I decided I had to put it out of my mind. Perhaps I'd even change my name: Oliver Capenter? Mungo Sniffer? Winston Derringer? Dick Nixon? Shirley Jones?

"Lance," I told the girl at the bar in Benton Harbor. She had been the local homecoming queen three years earlier, and her name was Mary Lou. She couldn't hack it in college and came home after two terms, had several jobs, and lost them all by oversleeping. She'd started at the Silver Cloud a month ago and thought it was all right because she didn't have to start work till five. I had four gin-and-tonics, the one drink I can consistently get down, and my tongue was loose and eloquent. The bar wasn't busy, and she lingered by my table. "I haven't seen you in here before. You're not from around here, are you?"

"No."

"Where you from?"

"Here and there." I remembered those Jack Palance-type westerns.

"Oh," she said, "Really? What do you do?"

·"Travel," was all I replied. Now I felt like Robert Mitchum.

"You don't talk much, do you?"

"Only when it's necessary. What time do you get off work?" Several dictionaries define a pot knight as a man made bold with drink. Actually I'm a blabbermouth.

"Well, usually one o'clock, but when it's not busy I can leave when I want to."

"Let's go."

"Where?"

"I don't know. Why don't you just take a chance?"

She hesitated. "Maybe I will. But give me time to change." She disappeared into the back of the tavern. A man about thirty-five came in and sat at the bar. He looked like a throwback to the black leather jacket days of 1955. Mary Lou came back wearing Levi's and a buckskin jacket with fringe. The Levi's made her long legs look even longer, and her ash-blonde hair hung straight down her back. She looked nervously at the fifties throwback as she walked past the bar. I got up and dropped a five-dollar bill on the table. I took her arm, and we walked toward the door.

I heard a voice behind me. "Hey, buddy, where do you think you're going?" I looked at Mary Lou, and her eyes were wide.

I turned around and saw the throwback half-sitting with one elbow on the bar, looking in our direction. I felt a light quaking in my knees. "Are you speaking to me?" I asked, quite calmly, I thought.

"Well, I ain't speaking to Mary Lou, and I don't see nobody else over there. Where do you think you're going with her?" I shot a quick glance at Mary Lou, and she looked up at me and whispered, "Cool it. He's trouble."

I was slightly shocked to hear myself say, "Out."

The throwback said, "I don't think so," and took another sip of his beer.

I held my right hand rigid in front of me as I'd seen it done on television and spread my feet just beyond the width of my shoulders. I saw myself up against a gray stone wall, a beret on the side of my head and a Thompson Invader submachine gun held at my waist, jerking violently and spitting smoky spent brass cases.

The throwback hesitated a moment, started to say something, then closed his mouth, turned back to the bar, and concentrated on his beer. I took Mary Lou's arm and walked out. I was shaky but tried not to let it show. In this age of closet karate, few men would call a good bluff; still, I felt uneasy as we walked to the car. I started the engine and we drove away. I looked in the mirror, but the street in front of the bar was empty and the light from the window cast no shadows on the snow-covered sidewalk. After a respectable silence I asked Mary Lou who the throwback was. "Lucas McGlue," she said. "He tries to impress me by humiliating strangers in the bar."

We drove around for a while and talked. We stopped at a bar in Three Rivers, and she told me about feeling trapped in Benton Harbor, how Lucas had continually bothered her and made her life miserable, how nobody had called his bluff before, about how she'd gotten engaged to his brother when she graduated from high school and then had doubts as to whether she really wanted to get married, about having the decision made for her when her fiancé was killed in Vietnam, how he'd been nothing like Lucas, but how Lucas felt it had fallen to him to protect her for the memory of his dead brother. I listened and told her I could understand, told her that I'd felt trapped too, felt my life had run out of possibilities, told her about my father's death, about leaving home, about having no plans but knowing I had to get away. By the time we left the bar she was lachrymose. She told me she thought I was beautiful and that my telling her about myself had almost made her want to cry.

The desk clerk at the Hoosier Guardian Motel, just off the Tri-State, was about twenty-five, the tall sallow type who would pick his nose in school and carry a briefcase. "Just staying the night?" he leered across the desk. "Got any bags?"

"Yes, we're just spending the night, and our luggage isn't any business of yours."

"I was just trying to make it easier for you, so you could pull around close to your room. You know, so you wouldn't have to carry your bags so far."

"I know what you meant," I said, "and my wife and I resent the implication, so if you'll just shut up and do your job, I'll overlook this incident and allow you to keep it."

He reached for the key and laid it quickly on the desk. "I'm sorry, sir, I really didn't mean anything. I was only, you know, trying to be helpful."

"Just show me where to sign," I said briskly and wrote "Mr. and Mrs. D. Hines, Jr.," as clearly as I could.

I guess it was walking toward the room that I first realized what I was doing. This was the first time in the ten years I'd been married to Gloria that I'd spent the whole night with another woman. There was one lamp burning between the twin queen-sized beds. Mary Lou sat

Indian-style on the end of the bed by the wall, and I put down the suitcase and closed the door. I took off my coat and sat by her on the bed. I thought I should say something but didn't know what it would be. Where to begin? I turned and kissed her, a short boyish peck at first. Her mouth opened, and she put one hand lightly on my shoulder. I was drawn toward her, leaning over her crossed legs. Her tongue played around my lips and teeth and then began searching the roof of my mouth. I was falling toward her, and she was falling along the length of the bed. Her legs opened, and I was lying between them. "What am I doing?" drifted quietly through my mind and was lost. I began kissing her neck, her hands ran up and down my back, and then my mouth was on her breast, at first through the blouse and then unbuttoning it, kissing her above the cotton bra. She pulled away for a moment, and the light went out. Her hands were on either side of my head, pushing it down to her breast, kissing in and around and through the bra as my hands felt behind her for the clasp. It was already undone. I lifted the bra and kissed a circle around one nipple and began sucking, running my tongue over the pink center, which began to stiffen. She began to move her lips and to breathe heavily through her mouth and through my hair. I moved down, kissing an imaginary line that divided her body, her hands cupped around my ears, followed my head, then pulled it gently back up to her lips. I unbuttoned her jeans; her hips moved toward me and I slipped my hand in, over the silk, the smooth mound padded softly with hair, that delicious curve through a soft fabric running slickly under my palm, the resilience of a thousand delicate springs, and beneath the silk, I know there's a God; that hump, that marvelous home, seen more clearly through a bathing suit or panties, more cleanly defined, *mons veneris,* that lovely word, requiring the tongue to tickle the roof of the mouth, to rasp forward lightly. My hand slid between her thighs, the warmth, heat really, and the dewy silk. She rolled her head slowly, and the faintest sound came from her throat. Her hands came back to my head, cradling it like a melon, then pushing it gently down, between her breasts, down the imaginary line, down to her navel, down to the soft white silk, her hands now on the top of my head, still pushing, coaxing, the tension of her body against my cheek, against my lips, a faint odor of perfume, no powder, it was powder and the damp of the silk against my lips. I pulled down the elastic at the top of her panties, kissing every inch of skin as it appeared, kissing the hair; and then the very edge of the flesh gave way under my lips, and her legs came over my shoulders, her breasts rising and falling and her arms over her head, holding the headboard.

3

Perhaps I should take a minute to talk about Gloria. We'd met when we were both students at Michigan State University, also known as M.S.U., Moo U., the Udder University, or by several other oblique references to its land-grant agricultural heritage. Gloria was from Birmingham, a fairly exclusive suburb of Detroit and a pasture land of middle executives, manufacturer's reps, junior V.P.s, in short, "men on the way up." Guy and Mimi, Gloria's parents, were on the way up to Bloomfield Hills, the final step in residential aggrandizement. Guy and Mimi were "regular guys." I'm not exactly sure what that means, but it's what my mother always said she wanted me to grow up to be, and everyone who met Guy and Mimi said they were "regular guys." I'm also not sure what a manufacturer's representative is, but that's what Guy was. I think it's some kind of a big-league, independent salesman who knows the "right people" and sells Kleenex dispensers and ash trays in million lots to Ford and G.M.

Though they still lived in Birmingham, Guy and Mimi Callahan belonged to the Bloomfield Hills Country Club, sort of getting their feet in the door to make the big move a little easier. They were in their middle forties when I was dating Gloria, and Guy was known as "the patent leather kid," partly because of his slick black hairdo, parted in the middle of his head, and partly because of his febrile ability to slip into any situation, club, or acquaintanceship that would further his career. Gloria was their only child; when she was grown, Mimi drank, played golf, and "cultivated" or I should say got plowed by Guy's business connections. As I mentioned before, I'd been in Detroit only three times.

Gloria was beautiful, like the blonde in the Breck Shampoo ad, though her chin seemed to jut out a little too far. At first she regretted having to leave the Detroit clusterfuck, but she soon took to life in Brainard. Our two children came after we'd been married five years; my pal and mistress became the devoted mother, a respectable matron, superb cook, and consummate housekeeper. I soon became a stranger, like the papa bear who'd planted his seed and was now only tolerated around the den. I drifted in and out of her life like a thin redundant fog, eating her cooking, disciplining her children, admiring her sense of order and her executive ability, and vaguely sharing her bed. The ideal marriage: "Father Knows Best," happy and boring.

It was some comfort knowing I wasn't causing misery by my absence. A few tears, a few inquiries, a sigh, and then life as usual with one familiar piece of furniture sent off to be reupholstered. I loved her, whatever that means.

But now there was Mary Lou, and it didn't take much talking to persuade her to become my traveling companion. No promises and no plans but the road ahead. I'd temporarily given up Rimbaud and Neruda, the standbys I'd disguised in *Business Week* covers and read at the office to maintain my sanity, for the *Rand McNally Road Atlas*, 44th annual edition. The Porsche wasn't due for service for another 8,000 miles, I had money, credit cards, and Mary Lou. I was, in short, equipped.

We stopped in Joliet to buy Mary Lou some bras, panties, and a toothbrush and headed out on Interstate 80,
across the flat farmland of northern Illinois, silo country.
I had a case full of eight-track tapes, and we alternated
Janis Joplin, Mary Lou's favorite, Judy Collins, Donovan,
and *Atom Heart Mother* by the Pink Floyd with excited
discussions of where we might go and what we might do.
Atom Heart Mother was especially helpful because it was
like an endless movie soundtrack. We smoked a little grass
and imagined we were driving through a Stanley Kramer
production. I remembered "Route 66" on TV in the early
sixties, Martin Milner and George Maharis, Buzz and
Tod, out to discover America in a Corvette Sting Ray. It
used to be my favorite program, not because it was particularly good, but it played out my fantasies, and that
made it marvelous.

And now it was all before me, and Mary Lou was better
company than Martin Milner, who'd given it all up to
become an L.A. TV cop. The snow began blowing across
the highway in the afternoon, and I helped eat up the
monotonous sea of Iowa by doing my imitations of hits
of the fifties, beginning with Bill Hailey and his Comets,
as introduced by Alan Freed, doing "Rock Around the
Clock," Little Richard's "Long Tall Sally," the Big Bop-
per's "Chantilly Lace"—"Hello baby, you knoooooow
what I like"—through Jimmy Rodgers' "Honey Comb,"
"Silhouettes," and "Lollipop," by I couldn't remember
who, Elvis's "Blue Suede Shoes" and "I Got a Woman,"
"Who Put the Bop in the Bop Shbop Shbop," "Get a Job,"
and finally Sam Cooke's sentimental favorite, "You ouu
ouu ouu Send Me." Mary Lou was laughing hysterically,
saying, "You're cra-a-azy," and my throat was raw and
aching; it brought tears to my eyes. The blower purred,
snow half-obscured the road, and we were coming into
Des Moines.

4

I don't know who taught Mary Lou her way around a man, but whoever it was, I'm grateful. I'd almost forgotten that it was possible to *make it* more than once in a night. I'm sure it was partly the sense of adventure, the miles ahead (through less than exotic lands), but knowing that she was pleased, that there was no notarized and stamped document binding her to my bed, the little noises she made and the heavy breathing were because of me, because I was touching her. I'd saved her from the prospect of another long and aimless winter in Benton Harbor, and she was grateful, but I wanted to believe it was more than that.

The sign was hard to see in the blowing snow as we approached the Holiday Inn. I glanced over at Mary Lou and said, "What do you think?" She slid her hand to my lap and cupped it softly around the bulge in my Levi's. Her head was back against the headrest. She laughed softly and said, "What do *you* think?"

We spent two nights in Des Moines, and didn't leave the motel much. We slept, watched TV, read magazines, ate, and, of course, made love. I remember the light from the window behind me, a small stream of light through a crack in the curtains, reflected in her eyes as I was fucking her the final time that night. Her head was raised slightly against the pillow, her eyes were open, and she was smiling at me. After I came, she contracted her vagina repeatedly around my cock like a milking machine, and I shivered. "Does that feel good?" she asked. I loved the feigned naïveté. "Are you kidding ," I whispered, falling to the pillow as if I'd just finished a hundred push-ups. She rolled me off her like a limp fish and lay full length on top of me. "You feel good," she said. "But I'm useless." I was wonderfully useless. "Never," she said, as I drifted off to sleep.

I remember a poem by Robert Frost called "The Roadside Stand," about farm people being gathered in from their difficult lives grubbing in the dirt, and being put on welfare. "And by letting them sleep all day, destroy their sleep at night, the ancient way." It seemed odd to think of Frost after making love, but the words "ancient sleep" kept running through my head, and I knew no more ancient sleep.

I'd better explain my allusions to poetry. I became addicted to Whitman as a sophomore in college, while taking an elective course in English. It was partly Whitman and partly the elegant lectures of Professor Claude Larimer. If anyone was responsible for destroying my stupidly happy and unquestioning life, Professor Larimer was the man. I was ensorcelled. For the first week of his class I groped to understand a word he said. He strutted back and forth across the room like a bull-elephant-sized peacock, his mouth spewing a seemingly endless stream of names and concepts, most of which I'd never heard before: Descartes, Boccaccio, Eliot, Chaucer, Hemingway, Swedenborg, Henry James, Ecclesiastes, and Terry Southern; Nabokov, Debussy, Chopin, Mahler, Thomas Mann, Michel de Montaigne, Whitman, of course, and on and on with occasional diversions into cordon-bleu cooking. I struggled and endured, and by the end of the term I was hooked. I got an A⁻ for the course. That shocked me. It was better than the grades I'd been getting in the Business Administration school where I'd been learning how to market Bancroft pies more competitively and efficiently in your local A&P.

I changed my major to English, careful to keep the news from my parents, though they didn't really pay too much attention. My father had started work when he was fourteen and was anxious for me to "Get out of school, graduate if you have to, but come back here and get your feet wet." I'd entertained vague notions about doing graduate work in comparative literature, but they were only vague. I'd been so thoroughly programmed that I never seriously considered the possibility of doing anything other than disappearing into the crust of the Bancroft Pie Company, though by the time I graduated, my head full of Whitman, Shakespeare, and Faulkner, I was destroyed for the world of business.

Frost also said, "The only certain freedom's in departure." How long it had taken me, and now only because the only man whose judgment mattered was dead.

The next morning Mary Lou and I took a shower together, packed, had breakfast in the coffee shop, and got back on 80 heading west. The storm had blown past, and it was clear and cold. The road was dry, with only a few patches of ice along the edges. It was good to be moving again through this winter desert, though now the country began to roll gently. A stream of freeway exits, gas stations, and invitations to "stop, or smile as you go by." Waukee, De Soto, Earlham, Dexter, "in love with the sound of American names," Casey, Adair, Amita, Marne, Walnut, Avoca, Hancock, Minden. I sounded them off like a Pullman porter and explained to Mary Lou about the old America, the one with trains.

5

In the long miles through eastern Nebraska I began to realize that Mary Lou was an extraordinarily beautiful girl. In all the excitement of the escape from the bar in Benton Harbor, the comatose state induced by the idea of making love to a strange girl, and the honeymoon that followed, I'd never really thought about it. We turned off the tape player and talked through Omaha and Lincoln. I told her about my wife and my son and daughter, about suffocation in the family business, in the whole life that had been prefabricated for me, about my attempts to write poetry, my brief foray into the world of sports-car racing where I'd won five of the eight races I'd run, been voted the outstanding novice driver of 1961, flattened myself against a concrete wall, breaking almost every bone in my body, and during my year of recovery been talked into giving it up by my wife and parents. The prodigal son with broken body and spirit, led meekly back to the farm. I told her of the years of faking it at the office, sneaking novels under my desk, the pointless repetitive jobs, okaying a million requisitions for the pickup of damaged pies, already approved by district sales managers in places and circumstances I knew nothing about; my disdain for golf and football outings, my love of skiing, motorcycles, and mountain climbing; how I'd climbed the Grand Teton in Jackson Hole, Wyoming when I was fourteen, running away from a summer ranch camp to go to mountaineering school, how my parents found out and for years afterward forbade me even books on mountain climbing; about being sent to a different school every year, my inability to "fit in," how I blackmailed my parents into letting me spend my senior year at Brainard High (the one good year I remembered) by threatening to join the Navy; about my corresponding with a poet I'd known casually in college and finding a life in his poems and letters.

But I said that Mary Lou was beautiful. The seats in the Porsche reclined, and she was half supine next to me, asleep and vulnerable. I'd decided she was beautiful while she was listening to the story of my life, asking just the right questions and being silent at the times to be silent. She told me about the life she was trying to escape, the future inevitable to so many girls in small towns, of being a waitress, secretary, or salesgirl until they married an arc welder or salesman and quickly grew old with children, neglect, and boredom, never having seen the world beyond fifty miles from home. The alternative was to not get married and become a dry spinster or the town punchboard, also aging quickly with boredom and neglect. Only a few who didn't go to college managed to get away, and she wanted to be one of them. She told me she liked to go to movies and thought *Dr. Zhivago* was her favorite. She'd read the novel after seeing the movie and found it difficult but was glad she'd finished it. She'd done the same with *Gone With the Wind* and *Romeo and Juliet*. I had the tape of the sound track of *Romeo and Juliet*, and we listened to it and got teary. She said she liked to read Pearl Buck and Mary Stewart novels that she borrowed from the library. Along with television, which she thought was mostly boring, and an occasional movie, they were her escape from the Silver Cloud. She liked *Midnight Cowboy* and *Five Easy Pieces* and had identified with Karen Black, though she thought she acted pretty dumb and could understand why Jack Nicholson treated her "as mean as he did." She talked about "wanting more out of life," but she wasn't sure what it was. I remembered that all the girls in my high school yearbook had wanted to "travel." It wasn't money, she said, though she wouldn't kick about having it. She could see it hadn't worked any miracles for me. Maybe it was just not wanting to know for sure where she'd be and what she'd be doing a year from now. I looked at her long legs stretched out next to me and intermittently glanced at her long blonde hair half-fallen over her face. I felt the worm stir in my Levi's and concentrated on the road.

Past the Army Ammunition storage mounds around Grand Island, the land began to erode. Under a thin cover of snow, western Nebraska and eastern Colorado looked like the surface of the moon, miles and miles of barren, eroded, brown earth, punctuated at what seemed extremely long intervals with a farmhouse, always surrounded by a three-sided wall of poplar trees, to protect it from the view of all that nothing. I wondered how people lived there.

While Mary Lou was sleeping, I was effectively alone for the first time since I'd met her. I thought about Gloria taking the children to school and picking them up, lunching at the club, planning menus, giving orders to the housekeeper, "bravely carrying on," and waited for the guilt feelings of adultery and desertion, but they didn't come. I remembered the great discovery I'd had the first time I read Blake's "The Marriage of Heaven and Hell."

I memorized "The Proverbs of Hell," many of which became slogans for the life I desired but was too timid to demand, temporarily liberating my spirit, though my body remained in its mundane, luxurious prison. "The road of excess leads to the palace of wisdom," "Prudence is a rich ugly old maid, courted by incapacity," "He who desires and acts not, breeds pestilence," "Prisons are built with the stones of law and brothels with the bricks of religion," and "Morality is a weakness of the brain." That last one was Rimbaud.

By now I would be a scandal in Brainard, the talk of the town. "Goddamn Arnie, I always knew the kid was a little weird. Remember when he got arrested in Chicago for smuggling booze on his high school 'skip trip,' and those letters and editorials he wrote in the paper about the war? I wouldn't be surprised if he's gone to Russia. I always thought he was a little pink. I don't know for sure, but I heard from a pretty reliable source that he was selling dope to the high school kids. Just up and left that pretty wife of his. Goddamn, I'd like to fuck her."

I decided if there was any morality, it resided in the ability to do certain things well, like the expertise involved in building the car I was driving or to a lesser degree my skill in driving it.

The best thing about the Porsche was that everything worked. After thirty-six thousand miles, many of them on rough country roads, the body was as tight as the day I bought it. The opposed six behind the rear wheels, the five-speed transmission, and the sloping nose of the car that reduced the frontal area to approximately that of an unfolded Miss January, made cruising at a minimum of eighty *de rigueur*, with, of course, a wary eye on the rearview mirror. Anything less seemed a criminal misuse of equipment, and besides it was boring. It had taken me a long time to come around to even seriously consider a Porsche. They had always emblemized a kind of precious "sporty car buff" I couldn't abide, the kind who always wore loden coats with wooden peg buttons, Porsche Club of America emblems, and Tyrolian hats adorned with a frosted shaving brush. Besides, I had a prejudice against Germans, instilled in the first six years of my life, the World War II years when I slept with a toy machine gun and woke up shooting "Krauts," particularly disturbing as my mother's ancestors came from Munich. But the Porsche was helping me overcome that, all that efficiency in a beautiful silver package, seventeen coats of enamel. The earlier Porsches had been designed strictly for function, but they had looked like a wheelbarrow full of assholes. If it's true that form follows function or form is merely an extension of content, the function and content had improved immeasurably; so had the heater, ventilating system, and weather stripping. The electrical system with twin twelve-volts and high-capacity discharge ignition had enough zap to send off the Rosenbergs. The salesman pointed to the black flap covering the left corner of the engine bay and said, "Stay out of there. That's charcoalsville." It made a deep impression. I suffer from electrophobia to the degree that I'm timid about changing the bulb in a flashlight. The image of an electric chair has always haunted my dreams. I had a recurring nightmare in which the state was going to fry my mother, and I was running up and down the dimly lit corridor that led to the death chamber, pleading for her life. Finally the lights grew even dimmer, and I woke up to a ripping sound like a Black and Decker rotary saw biting into a piece of three-quarter-inch pine.

I remember my revulsion the summer they executed the Rosenbergs, the cold, calculated, passionless ritual of death, officially sanctioned death, the intricate descriptions in the *Chicago Tribune*, the fact that they both chose fried onions for their last meal, the image of the fried onions frying again. When I was fourteen I read *Cell 2455 Death Row*, and Caryl Chessman became a household word and secret hero. I was numb with disbelief when the guards and prison officials he'd lived with for fourteen years led him to a little green steel room, strapped him into the left-hand chair, and looked at him through the windows as they filled his lungs with cyanide. I wonder if they waved good-bye to him, I wonder what expression he had on his face and if he tried to tell them something. I wonder what the guards said to their wives and children when they went home: "Well, we put Caryl away last night," like a veterinarian who'd just put an old dog out of its pain.

But, as I was saying, the Porsche worked. It emanated confidence and well-being and instilled the belief that nothing wrong could happen here. Maybe it was that sense of security that made the Germans think they could conquer the world. Maybe the Porsche (or the Volkswagen) is the reason that stereo-typed Germans are always laughing and slapping their lederhosened thighs. Maybe it's just the fact that so many Americans buy them.

6

I left Mary Lou at the Denver Holiday Inn near Stapleton Airport to wash her hair, while I drove to a gas station to get the Porsche washed. We'd picked up a lot of lanolin, dandruff, road grit, and salt in Nebraska. Everyone was busy at the gas station, but the wash-bay was free, and the manager told me I could use his equipment and wash it myself for seventy-five cents. Scrubbing the wheels reminded me of working at Ben Flatt's Mobil station. "Go out and get a job," my father said when I was fourteen. "Build character, learn the value of a dollar, and get off your dead ass." I started out as washboy, and my first job was a Bell Telephone pole-setting truck, covered with tar and creosote. It took me all day to get it clean, and since it was piecework, I was paid one dollar and twenty-five cents, really starting at the bottom. I'd always wanted to work in a gas station, mostly for the glamor—the dreams of all the beautiful girls I'd meet and impress with my skill in pumping gas and my extensive knowledge of low-detergent oils. Ma Bell popped my balloon with her cruddy truck, and it was a year before I advanced to the pumping platoon; by that time, except for Ben's stories and boxing lessons, it was just a job.

We went to dinner at the Harum Scarum, a supper club which as it turned out was also a whorehouse. Lots of obtrusive Rita Hayworth types alone at the bar and at tables around the room. The headwaiter would seat an unaccompanied man at a table with one of the girls, and a seemingly constant flow of drinks, cigarettes, sandwiches, and flowers would be brought to the table. Occasionally a newly attached couple would leave their table and walk back toward the rest rooms together. In fifteen or twenty minutes the man would emerge, slip a bill to the waiter, get his coat, and leave; and the Rita, looking none the worse for wear, would go back to her table, which had been cleared for a new victim. I was fascinated. So was Mary Lou. The idea of a man paying for all those drinks and cigarettes plus whatever he paid in the back room to jack-off in some hooker's box struck her as too funny to be believed, and I was afraid her near-hysterical laughter was going to get us ejected. As it turned out, we were driven out by Denny Condon, the floor show, a local Bobby Darin-Tom Jones type with lots of finger snapping and "ya, ya's" to "That Old Black Magic," "It's Not Unusual," and "I Got You Under My Skin," doubtless the theme song of the girl at the newly cleared table.

We'd decided on Aspen and got an early start. I'd been there before with Gloria, and Mary Lou said she'd always wanted to try skiing. We had to go somewhere. It was overcast as we headed into the mountains, leaving Denver below in a temperature-inversion bank of smog. A light snow started falling when we'd made Idaho Springs, and by the time we got to Loveland Pass it was a howling blizzard. I put on the chains, and we started the long climb, fishtailing and scratching for traction all the way up. Near the top we caught up with a Mayflower Van truck, and passing was out of the question. As we broke out on the ridge, the truck disappeared in the blowing snow; then the front of the Porsche disappeared. All I could see were two useless windshield wipers rhythmically sweeping the glass against a background so bright that even with my sunglasses on I had to squint. We were experiencing what the natives called a "white-out," and there was nothing to do but keep the heater running and hope that we didn't run out of gas before visibility returned. We sat in silence for a long while, half hypnotized by the steady thump of the wipers, the whirr of the blower, and the constant impenetrable white. I remember that Melville devoted an entire chapter of *Moby Dick* to the pristine terror of white, the deadly innocent color of the polar bear, the great white shark (called *requin* by the French, short for *Requiem Eternum*), the white whale, of course, and the avalanche. Fortunately we were at the top of the pass; I knew that cars had been swept off the roads by the weight of sliding snow and that every winter several skiers were lost, usually in deep powder areas beyond the groomed trails. One year I'd volunteered for a search team to look for the body of a skier who'd disappeared on the far side of Aspen Mountain. We probed for five days with long steel rods, but only found his ski poles, a half mile apart. His body turned up in June, still well preserved, at the bottom of the valley where it had lain under forty feet of snow. I told Mary Lou about it, and she said she wasn't so sure she wanted to try skiing after all. I told her that very few people were swept away on the bunny runs. She shoved in a Simon and Garfunkel tape, and we listened to "Bridge Over Troubled Waters" and an imitation of the Everly Brothers doing "Bye Bye Love." I wished that they'd do "Wake Up Little Susie," but I realized that nostalgia wouldn't make the "magic black sound box" transcend its programmed limits.

As the music faded into recorded applause, I heard someone knocking on the window. When I cranked it down, I could see a thin woman, about fifty, with a purple felt hat. She looked like a refugee from a bake sale.

"Could you move your car so we could get by?" she asked in her squeaky nasal voice. I looked ahead and still couldn't see my own headlight rims.

"Where do you suggest I move it?"

"Well, just pull it over to the side. You just can't park in the middle of the road, you know."

"Madam, if you'll grope a few feet past the hood of my car, you'll find a Mayflower Van Lines truck that isn't going to move; and if you'll grope your way a few feet to the right of my car, you'll find eternity off the edge of a thousand-foot cliff."

"Well, there ought to be a law about this," she said, shaking her head.

"There is. It was passed by Newton, and it's called the law of gravity, and if you don't want to test it I suggest you go back to your car and sit on your shift lever."

Her eyes and mouth were wide, but her words were lost in the wind and in the window glass climbing shut. Scene Two.

"You didn't need to be quite so harsh with that poor bitch," Mary Lou said.

I suggested that she mind her own business, too, and then apologized. I've known of people who'd gotten hung up in Loveland Pass for as long as twenty-four hours; and if we were going to be in any condition to drive when it cleared, we'd have to keep our cool.

The wind let up about three o'clock, and I could see the signs on the back of the Mayflower Van: "We pay $2,560.00 per year in Highway Taxes," and "America, Love it or Leave it." "Goddamn Arnie, pass the Pepto Bismol. I bought America again today, and you're going to enjoy it whether you like it or not. No commie pinko preevert's going to try to tell me it ain't swell." The truck driver was always played by Slim Pickens. I recalled the ingenious counterpart to the ubiquitous "Love it or Leave it" sign, "Put your heart in this country or get your ass out of it," with a valentine heart and the symbol of the Democratic Party substituted for the respective nouns, on the back of a pickup camper I was following the previous deer season in Michigan. The men in the camper expressed their love by decorating the roadside with aluminum beer cans. I'd noticed that the pickup also had a trailer hitch, doubtless to pull a snowmobile in December.

The Mayflower Van pulled away, and I released the hand brake and put the Porsche in gear. After several hours of sliding down mountains and planing through ponds of slush in the valleys, we stopped in Vail for gas, windshield-washer solvent, and a cup of coffee. Mary Lou had a cheeseburger with everything but, and I took three Excedrin. It was close to seven-thirty when we pulled into Aspen, checked in at the Villa Motel on the edge of town, and drove over to the Chart House for a steak, an artichoke, and a half-dozen drinks each. We got rapidly blotto in our new high-altitude environment, crawled back to the Villa, half undressed, and fell asleep with one hand on the wall and one foot on the floor, the room spinning like a Stanley Kubrick special effect.

7

I had a dream in which Gloria married Kirk Douglas. They met by correspondence and exchanged wallet-sized photos like pen pals. The wedding took place in the same church in which Gloria and I were married. I was the best man. After the wedding we all went out to lunch together and then drove Kirk to the airport where he caught a plane back to Hollywood. Everyone waved good-bye, and that was the end of it. It all seemed perfectly natural. The plane disappeared off the end of the runway, and I went home with Gloria. Nothing more was said about it.

In the morning while Mary Lou was still sleeping and I was recovering from my astonishment at not having a hangover, I arranged to rent a small condominium above the Paragon restaurant and bar. I'd rigged a cache for my money belt under the seat of the Porsche, and before leaving the motel, I scanned the locale to make sure no one was watching, removed ten one-hundred-dollar bills and folded them into my shirt pocket. Aspen was expensive, full of good restaurants and lousy with equipment.

The first thing we had to do was get outfitted for skiing. It was a clear cold day. All the tourists were taking advantage of it on the slopes, and the streets seemed relatively empty. I found a parking place right in front of the Cripple Creek Ski Company. It seems silly to worry about traffic congestion in a small town in the Rockies, but if I have to park two blocks away from where I'm going, I feel put upon. I started looking over the skis, and Mary Lou headed straight for the stretch pants department, lost in the dazzle of pink and chartreuse parkas, sweaters, nylon windshirts, hip-huggers, and hot pants.

I was flexing a pair of VR 17's when I heard a voice behind me. "Hey, mister, if you break it, you buy it." I turned around and saw Ozzie Pierce.

"Ozzie."

"Hey, man, what are you doing in Aspen? I thought they kept you tied up in the pie mill."

"Well, Jesus, Ozzie, that's a long story."

"Did you bring Gloria with you?"

"Well, no, I didn't."

"Did you come alone?"

"Well, not exactly. Like I said, it's a long story." It was the first time I'd confronted anyone from my predeparture existence, my first accounting for the best week of my life, and it was slightly uncomfortable. Ozzie had known Gloria in school, and he and his wife, Sandy, had been frequent skiing and dinner companions on our visits to Aspen.

"I came with someone else, another girl."

"Hey, man, that's kind of heavy. Maybe you don't want to talk about it."

"No, Ozzie, as a matter of fact I do. I'd like to talk about it because I haven't really thought about it. But what are you doing here? I thought you were instructing over at Snowmass."

"I was, but it got old fast, and I had an opportunity to buy into this place. It was too good to pass up."

"Why don't we go someplace and have a cup of coffee?"

"Okay. One nice thing about being the boss is I can take off when I want to."

"Wait a minute. See that girl over by the stretch pants rack?" I pointed to Mary Lou. "That's the one."

Ozzie flushed and ran his hand through his hair. "Goddamn, Larry, you don't waste time, do you?"

"She's better than a kick in the ass. Let me tell her we're going; I'll introduce you later."

We walked to a little restaurant around the corner, a converted store with a glass front, bare wood floors, and brick walls, decorated in an "Old West saloon" motif, with potted ferns hanging from the rough-hewn crossbeams, skiing photos, and watercolors on the walls. I feigned a lot of interest in Ozzie's business and let him talk about it. It was easier that way. "It's a gold mine," he said. "People who come to Aspen spend money like they think the world is going to end. My biggest problem is keeping things in stock: skis, boots, poles, clothes, sunglasses, lip balm; and the crowd changes about every week, so I get a whole new wave of consumers. They all want to become bronzed ski gods. But what about you? Goddamn, man, I figured you'd go crazy in the straitjacket they built for you back in Brainard, but I'm surprised it took this long. What's the story with Gloria, I mean of course if you want to talk about it."

"My father's dead" was all that came out.

"Oh. I'm sorry. Was it sudden? I mean, he hadn't been sick, had he?"

"No. A heart attack. He just died in his sleep. He was seventy-four years old, and he still went to the office every day. Then he just came home, had dinner and a couple of drinks with my mother, played with his electric trains, went to bed, and died. It really couldn't have been better, or something like that."

"When did it happen?"

"About ten days ago."

"And you just took off?"

"I tried to comfort my mother. I made the arrangements for the funeral and then walked right out on the service, on the preacher trying to explain that he wasn't really dead, on everyone weeping and telling each other it was God's will and all for the best." I was talking through clenched jaws and lightly pounding the table by the time I got to the end of the sentence. "I guess my father was the only thing that was holding me there. He always told me that just because he wanted me to come back and work for the company didn't necessarily make it the thing I ought to do. It was the rest of the family that put the pressure on, told me I'd break his heart if I gave it all up. Well, it broke anyway. It was a long time, but I just couldn't tell him. I had to wait for him to die." I could feel the tears on my cheeks. They were hot, and my face was flushed. "I worked for him, had dinner with him once in a while, and waited for him to die." I wiped my face with the palm of my hand and the sleeve of my sweater. "I guess this is the first time I've really known he's dead. Anyway, I gave up the whole thing: my job, Gloria and the kids, everything."

Ozzie was scratching designs in the place mat with his spoon. "What are you planning to do?"

"I don't have any plans, at least not yet, and I don't want any. I'm just going to keep moving for a while."

"What about Gloria?"

"What about Gloria? She's beautiful and I love her, I guess. I tell her I do. I love the kids, too, but I just don't want to think about them. I've been going to write a letter, but I just don't want to have to think about what I'll say." The coffee was cold, and I hadn't touched it. We ordered two fresh cups and agreed to go skiing together. We agreed to get together for dinner, too, but not for a couple of days. I wanted to cool off a little and have some fun before I confronted Sandy.

Ozzie left some change on the table, and we walked back to the store. I introduced Ozzie as an old friend from school and Mary Lou as just "Mary Lou." She'd picked out navy-blue over-the-boot ski pants, a pink-and-green-flowered wind shirt, a blue sweater, and a hot-pink parka. She'd fit right in. I suggested that she get some long underwear, ski socks, and a hat. She said she hadn't thought of that. The Silver Cloud Bar in Benton Harbor, Michigan, seemed years away.

The next morning Ozzie and I dropped Mary Lou off at Buttermilk Mountain and enrolled her in the ski school. She looked like a native in her ski clothes, though there was a certain reserve in her voice when she said good-bye. I kissed her and told her to relax and have fun. I told her she couldn't get hurt if she didn't tense up, a white lie, and that we'd pick her up at four o'clock. She didn't really look enthusiastic.

Ozzie and I drove out to Snowmass. After two runs from halfway up, we decided it was too cold to ski and went in for an hour-long coffee break. We talked about the ski business, the rapid development of ski-boot technology, and the superior training of the French Ski Team and their unorthodox racing techniques. We talked about fly fishing and the sexual revolution. We finished our third cup of coffee and went back to the slopes. The sun had come out, and it had warmed considerably. We made one run from the top of Big Burn and stopped at the Oyster Bar for a lunch of dark beer and a dozen bluepoints each. It occurred to me that if I were back in Brainard I'd be sitting at my desk, cursing the fact that it was only three o'clock and not five, precisely what I must have been doing two weeks earlier in another life.

We made two more runs after lunch, and my legs finally started working. The rhythm began to develop, and my knees were pumping like Koni shock absorbers. The bumps seemed to disappear, and my skis found their way through the moguls like a snake. I didn't want to stop, but the sun had dropped below the rim of the mountain, and the temperature with it. On the last run, the thermometer at the top registered ten below, and my nose and cheeks were numb.

Mary Lou said that her instructor was "cute" but he was German and she could hardly understand him. "They're infiltrating," I thought. She did make out that he'd said she seemed to have a lot of natural ability, but I already knew that.

We were invited to Ozzie's house for dinner. The confrontation with Sandy wasn't as bad as I'd feared. Ozzie had prepared her, and though she was a little reserved at first she loosened up when Mary Lou offered to help her wash the dishes. Ozzie brought out his supply of dope, and the course of the evening changed radically. We had hash brownies for dessert and sat on the floor listening to the music from *2001*, smoking grass and drinking Boone's Farm Apple Wine. Sandy gave me several nose hits by putting the lighted end of the joint in her mouth and blowing the smoke up my nose. I found the position and the eye contact particularly erotic. The room began to glow and then seemed to be drifting through space, pulled by the soprano voices and electronic sounds from the record player. Stars and planets and asteroids passed, and we talked about the idea of infinity being at the same time obvious and incomprehensible, how moon walks had become boring but had at least allowed us to see the Earth as a foreign planet, as one big blue-and-white milky marbled ball. Sandy wondered if that was the same thing as aesthetic distance, and I said I guessed it was, seeing the Earth as if it wasn't ours, thinking of the Earth as just another planet and not just something to walk on. We talked about the possibility of other intelligent life in the universe, and Ozzie expounded on the mathematical probability that an infinite number of stars that were merely suns more distant than our own, presumably each with its own planets and solar system, had to provide for other intelligent life, although the distance to the nearest star was too great for us to comprehend, let alone travel. Ozzie read *Newsweek* and a lot of Loren Eiseley. Sandy was rolling her head on the back of the couch and saying, "Oh, wow," and "Too-oo much." Infinity had overpowered us.

I switched on the television, and Billy Graham's cracker face and washboard hairdo filled the screen. He was crusading in Dallas and asking us to "come to me and take Jesus into your heart as your own personal savior." A personalized Jesus, what an idea, a packaging redesign. He could have his hair styled and wear a tuxedo like Englebert Humperdinck. Maybe a first name would help: Don Jesus or Duane Jesus. "My name's Buddy Jesus, but you can call me Bud." A Jesus leitmotif, scored by Leonard Bernstein, your own special Jewish Jesus symphonizer from Kennedy Center.

The fact that a woman wants me to fondle her most intimate parts, wants to kiss and caress mine, wants to share all that pleasure, wants to initiate it all, still delights and amazes me. When we returned from Ozzie's, Mary Lou went back to the bedroom, and I collapsed in a chair and switched on the Johnny Carson show. David Steinberg was substituting for Carson and having a difficult time getting anything going with Amy Vanderbilt, who sat there smiling with her lower lip like a rubber beach toy.

"La-a-arry," Mary Lou sang from the bedroom.

"What do you want?" I shouted.

"Come here a minute."

"Okay."

I walked back to the bedroom and stopped in the doorway. It took a moment for my eyes to adjust to the half-light of the street, strained through the curtains. As the blackness began to fade, I could see her outline on the bed and then the outlines of the black lace bra and panties against her skin. I dropped my clothes on the floor. Later I remember her long blonde hair sweeping over my stomach and pelvis and the voice of Ed McMahon bellowing somewhere far away.

8

It was time to write a letter to Gloria. I at least had to let her know I was alive; it hadn't been her fault I'd mucked up my life. I drove Mary Lou to Buttermilk for her ski school and came back to the apartment, made a cup of instant coffee, and set it on the kitchen table. I found some ruled notebook paper in a desk drawer in the living room, I drank the coffee and watched the chair lift at Little Nell haul bodies up the mountain. It was a Saturday in late February, and every chair was filled. I sat down and placed a sheet of paper on top of a copy of *Sports Illustrated*.

Dear Gloria:

I don't know how to begin. I don't know exactly why I left, but I had to. I just want you to know that I'm all right. I miss you and the children, but I can't come home yet. If I did, nothing would be solved. It would be like volunteering to return to an illness—not you and the children, I don't mean that—but my whole life, the life I've been living that wasn't mine, like trying to wear a suit of clothes tailored for my father. You can tell my mother you heard from me if you like. I guess if it hadn't been for my father, I would have done this a long time ago. I cleaned out the bank account—money for a new start, or a grubstake to look for it anyway. The savings account book is in the kitchen drawer. It's in our names jointly so you can withdraw what you need, all of it if you like.

Don't try to find me. I'm not in Aspen. I mailed this letter to Ozzie Pierce and asked him to post it for me. It's been little more than a week, but it seems longer and, at the same time, not long enough. I'll write again. I'm not sure where I'm going or what I'll do, but I'm well.

Love,
Larry

I folded the paper carefully, put it in an envelope, and sealed it. I wasn't sure it said what I really wanted to say, but at least it was done. I walked down to the post office, bought a stamp, which I pasted on upside down, and mailed it. Walking back I felt a little silly about the stamp. It was the way we'd stamped our letters when we were separated during the summers we were in college. But it was over, and I felt as if I'd just completed a difficult exam. I didn't know if I'd passed, but it was over.

I stopped at the Aspen Book Shop to buy a copy of Volume IV of the Diary of Anaïs Nin and went back to the apartment. I spent the afternoon reading about the kind of life I'd wanted to lead, the kind of people I wished I'd known, people who had something more than the moment and their plans for tomorrow.

I took Mary Lou to Andre's for dinner. We were seated at a dimly lit table at the back of the building and had sherry while ordering, several glasses of sherry. It was cozy, and the warmth of the sherry and the anticipation of roast duck with orange sauce made me feel alive and generous. We talked about Mary Lou's skiing, how she was already well into stem christies, and how her instructor, an American this time, had asked her for a date. I felt a twinge of jealousy, and then reflected that if it had been Gloria, I would have been flattered that she had been asked and let it go at that.

"What did you tell him?" I asked.

"I told him yes, of course," she replied.

"Oh, good. When are you meeting him?"

"After dinner. He's picking me up at the apartment." She must have seen something in my face, because she quickly added, "No, I'm just kidding. I told him my daddy wouldn't let me date ski instructors. Besides, he has bad breath."

"You could take him a bottle of Scope," I suggested.

"He has acne too."

"Terminal acne?"

"Terminal."

"Then there's no hope. We'll lave him in calamine lotion and freeze him until there's a major medical breakthrough."

"A good idea." She hesitated a moment and toyed with her sherry glass. "Larry." Another pause. "What about us?"

"What about us?"

"I mean, what's going to happen to us?"

"Jesus Christ, Mary Lou, I haven't got a crystal ball. I don't know what's going to happen to me, let alone us. Can't you let it go at that?"

"I'm sorry. I guess I just like being with you, and I don't want it to stop. You don't have to yell at me."

"I'm sorry, Mary Lou. I just wrote a letter to Gloria, I mean my wife, and I feel like I've done enough accounting for one day."

"Do you think you'll go back to her?"

"I told you, I don't know what I'm going to do. I've had a very unusual week in my life, and I don't know what's going to happen. It's been a good week too, and I'd just like it to continue. When it's time to go, we'll go. Just how far we'll go, I don't have any idea." There was an intermission while the waiter served the roast duck.

"Larry, I'm sorry I brought it up. I'm just happy to be with you, and we'll let it go at that. Okay?"

I reached for her hand and kissed it. "Your duck's getting cold," she said.

After dinner we went across the street to Danny's Bar to have a few drinks and dance to the Nitty Gritty Dirt Band. Even in the Aspen world of beautiful people where everybody looks like either the *Rolling Stone* or *Town & Country*, Mary Lou was outstanding, and now with a little sun on her face she turned heads everywhere we went. Why she felt she was trapped in Benton Harbor is something I'll never understand, though I remembered that frequently, in school, the most attractive girls went dateless. I think that beautiful women intimidate men, and no potential Lothario can believe that they aren't already booked solid or would, in any case, be interested in him. Afraid of certain rejection, they pull in their horns and the Candice Bergens and Cybill Shepherds sit home and earn good grades.

I was just finishing my second gin-and-tonic when I heard a German accent asking Mary Lou to dance. I looked up and saw an immense blond ski god with styled hair.

"I don't think so, but thanks," said Mary Lou.

"You are really mizzing something," the ski god insisted, resting his hand on her shoulder.

I felt the fur rise along my spine. "The lady said she didn't want to dance, and I'll thank you to keep your hands off her." My words sounded slow and protracted, as if John Wayne were speaking them. Maybe it was the cowboy boots I was wearing, but I imagined I looked like John Wayne, The Duke.

"Who is zis?" the ski god asked Mary Lou.

"I happen to be the man she's with."

"You happen to be za man she *vas* with," he said and looked again at Mary Lou. "I repeat my offer to rescue you from zis boredom." He nodded toward The Duke as he emphasized the word "boredom."

"I don't think so," Mary Lou said.

"But I inzist."

"If you don't fuck off," I heard The Duke say, "I'm going to ship you back to Berlin." I couldn't believe my ears. Didn't The Duke realize this wasn't a movie, that there wasn't a stunt man to take his place. This time he'd gone too far. My heart was pounding, and I felt a familiar trembling in my knees. The ski god reached for The Duke's sweater and pulled him slowly to his feet.

"You Americans theenk you own everything," he said. "Well, I'm going to teach you za price vor shooting off your mouth."

The Duke felt his right arm cock like a hand trap. The Messerschmitts were dive-bombing and he coolly fixed them in the crosshairs of his pom-pom gun. The trap sprung, and I felt a sharp pain across my knuckles. The ski god crashed into the next table and lay motionless on the floor. I was amazed. There seemed to be an almost endless breaking of glasses, and a fat lady in ski pants sat in the corner screaming. The band played "Santa Rosa."

I felt a hand on my shoulder and turned my head. It was the bartender.

"Look, I don't want any trouble here," he said. "I'm going to have to ask you to leave."

"Okay, fine," I said, still dazed at the ease with which the ski god flew backward. It was the first time I'd hit anyone since high school. "What do I owe you for the drinks?"

"For settling his hash, it's on the house," he said, patting me on the shoulder. "Come back anytime, but not tonight, okay?"

We stopped at the drugstore for some iodine and bandages for my hand and walked across the street to the apartment. "It must have been his teeth," I said, as Mary Lou wound the gauze.

9

On the third lap I went deep into turn nine and took the leader on the inside. He settled in behind me, and we swept through the long curve like the Panama Limited, drifting wide to the edge of the wall. Coming out of the turn, it happened. I was dropping down off the slope of the turn when I felt the nudge, as if someone touched my shoulder. The white car filled my mirrors. I was going sideway, out of control. I reversed the steering wheel, but nothing happened; then I was spinning, and the pit wall was coming up fast. It was exhilarating, for a moment, then everything slowed down. I could see the wall moving slowly toward me; the concrete was porous. I could see the little holes in the wall. When the impact came, the car compressed like an accordion. I stopped breathing, my face shot forward into the steering column, and my hands ripped the steering wheel rim off the spokes. My nose covered my eye like a patch, and the air was full of glass and fire, the engine against my right shoulder. I was sailing backward; then another thud, and I was spinning again. The pits drifted past the space where my windshield had been. Some people were running, and some stood dumbly with their hands in the air. Then I was looking back down the track, and another car was closing fast. He swerved, another impact, and I was spinning in the opposite direction. All I could see was fire, and I wanted out. Everything stopped. I pulled the latch on my lap to release the belt and rolled onto the track. The air was full of smoke and vapor from the CO_2 bottles. I was drowning. I struggled for the surface, but there was no air. I was choking on blood, and I saw Gloria. I tried to tell her I was dying, but nothing came out, and it didn't matter. You're dying, I thought. That's too bad.

The doctors were standing in a circle above me, and there was a light in the center. They were busily handing instruments back and forth and sewing. Then they stopped. They looked so solemn. I wanted to cheer them up.

"Don't anybody laugh," I said, imitating Mickey Rooney. No response.

"Hey, I'm still here," I shouted. A policeman's head poked into the circle.

"I've got to ask some questions."

I heard a deep voice say, "I'm sorry, you're too late," and a white sheet fell over my face.

I sat up in bed, the sheet wrapped around my hand. The room was unfamiliar. There was a strange girl lying next to me. I got out of the bed, and the walls struck out at me, and the street lights shone through the curtains. I was listening to Beethoven's Wellington Symphony, as if through stereo headphones, the drums imitating cannons, firing back and forth across the orchestra, firing at each other through the battleground of my head. I removed myself from the headset and pressed the earpieces together so the cannons could fire directly into each other's mouths, the two halves of the orchestra crashing head-on, the infinite rooms of sound, like the infinite

Larry Bancrofts standing between the facing mirrors in my parents' bedroom, as if I were a revenant from my childhood.

"Aspen, Aspen, Colorado, February 1972." My mouth was dry, and I couldn't breathe through my nose. I looked at Mary Lou. I leaned over and kissed her, and she smelled like sleep. I went to the bathroom and took a leak, had a glass of water, and blew my nose. My hand was throbbing slightly, and then I remembered the fight. My nightshirt was damp with perspiration. I took it off and hung it over the shower rail. I looked at my face in the mirror and admired the job the surgeons had done on my nose and chin. I filled the glass again, took two Librium, and returned to a vacant world of sleep.

I woke up late and smelled coffee. I listened to Mary Lou in the kitchen and watched a light snow falling against the grey sky. I called Mary Lou and told her I'd had a bad dream. She unbuttoned her blouse and fell on the bed. We made love twice; the second time she was pumping her legs, raking my ribs and hips with her thighs, and moaning so loud I thought the neighbors would hear. Who cares? She wrapped her arms and legs around me and contracted her vagina. I thought my head would blow off. Then she relaxed, and we lay together for a long time and didn't speak. The snow was still falling, and the hot-air register ticked. I smelled something slightly acrid.

"I'll bet the bacon is ruined," she said. We took a shower together and had a leisurely breakfast. It was two o'clock in the afternoon.

10

The country club in Brainard is located on Goosepoint Road and therefore called the Goosepoint Country Club. Gloria was president of the club's distaff organization, known jejunely as "The Goslings." When I asked her why it wasn't more aptly called "The Honkerettes," she told me to shut up and said that if I would become more "involved" I wouldn't feel the juvenile impulse to ridicule.

It would be five o'clock in Brainard, and I would be leaving the office. The beech and hemlock around the house would be covered with snow, and I'd have to try three times to make the electric garage-door-opener work. Gloria would tell me the latest gossip about Sally Travis, her rival for supremacy in The Goslings, and then complain that the garbage disposal wasn't working. I wonder what Gloria is doing right now, I thought. I wonder if she's filed for divorce; maybe she's gone to the police, maybe there are bulletins out on me: a burglary committed the night I left town, they'd implicated me, *Wanted for inter-state flight to avoid prosecution.* I considered going back to the post office but decided that would be going too far. What is Gloria up to?

There are moments that have a redeeming value inherent in their own awfulness, moments that can make you flush ten years later, if memory hasn't been merciful enough to obliterate them. My memory is seldom merciful. I remember the most unsavory events with pellucid clarity, all the way back to sitting in the middle of a warm and ever-widening puddle during story hour in the first grade, because I was afraid Miss Chatham would get mad if I asked for permission to go to the toilet—events that remind me that my real forte is fucking up. The Catholic School I vandalized when I was seven, the vines I "cleaned" off my grandfather's house when I was five, and the high school graduation ceremony I was prevented from participating in because I was in jail on a drunk and disorderly charge, the one time in my life. No, I take that back. I always found it necessary to choke down as much booze as I could before going to a family soirée, those full-dress dinners when my mother broke out her best crystal and china and everyone glutted themselves on canapés and played *Who's Afraid of Virginia Woolf.* One of these inquisitions was to be particularly auspicious because of the presence of Senator Ralph Vanderplog, an old friend of my father's, and Mrs. Vanderplog, who shared with my mother a rapacious interest in those noxious pictures of big-eyed children. I had three gin-and-tonics, followed by an entire bottle of Bristol Cream. The second half of the bottle was easy. With that kind of fuel I was sure to be above the fray. Gloria half-led me to the door which I pounded, shouting, "Open in the name of God and the Continental Congress." I'd read that somewhere.

"Oh God, Larry," Gloria said, "not again."

My mother turned to Mrs. Vanderplog, smiled weakly and said, "Oh, that Larry's such a nut."

Someone took my coat and led me into the living room where my father said, "Senator Vanderplog, this is my son Larry."

"Senator," I said in my best business voice, shaking hands. I was then led to Mrs. Vanderplog, and my mother said, "Mrs. Vanderplog, may I present my son, Larry."

Mrs. Vanderplog offered her hand, and I kissed it, bowed, and said, "My being pulses pitzocotta with hosannas." But something was breaking loose. I weaved forward, dropping her hand, and laid my head on her shoulder. This was it; I was fading fast. I melted to my knees, my head sliding down her decolletage. Her hands were in the air, as if she were being held up.

"I'm sorry," I said mildly, lurched forward and vomited an entire bottle of sherry on her shoes.

It seemed I'd done it again there in Aspen. Ozzie called about two-thirty. "Hey, macho, what are ya doin?"

"What do you mean, 'macho'?" I asked.

"The whole town's talking about you. You're either a hero or a marked man."

"What are you talking about?"

"Last night, Danny's Bar."

"Yeh. I remember a little fuss with some German." I was being modest.

"Some German. Do you know who that was? That was Gunther Henken."

"So who's Gunther Henken?" I asked.

"Gunther Henken just happens to be Billy Badass around this town, and nobody messes with him, nobody but you that is. You busted his jaw."

"I never busted a jaw in my life," I said, surprised and a little pleased.

"Well you have now, and you picked the wrong one to

bust. Gunther Henken is known as 'Gunther the Terrible.' He dismembers people for amusement."

"Isn't there a law against that?" I asked.

"Sure there is. It's called assault with a deadly weapon,
Gunther himself being the weapon, but the police are
afraid of him. And he's got lieutenants, too."

"Jesus Christ, Ozzie, are you putting me on?"

"No, man, I'm just calling to warn you. Gunther's in
the hospital for a few days, but he's vowed revenge. So
if you haven't got another one of those Sunday punches
handy, you'd better disappear."

"Thanks, Ozzie," I said, dazed.

"Get out while you're ahead. Leave town a hero or stay
and be a victim. I'll do anything I can to help, but don't
take too long to think about it."

"Thanks, Ozzie." I hung up the phone and looked up
at Mary Lou. "Guess what," I said.

I'm a storehouse of inaccurate statistics. I can manufac-
ture statistics to suit my mood, to shock my mother-in-
law, or to reinforce my prejudices—the gratuitous lie,
unearned, unexpected, and therefore, believed:

1. John Keats was only 4'11" tall (true).
2. Francis Bacon had three testicles. (I'm not sure
   about this one.)
3. Abstinence is the most frequent cause of schizo-
   phrenia and ringworm.
4. The chances of my repeating last night's performance were precisely 3,721.02 to 1.

And this most immediate statistic:

5. If I didn't get out of town my chances of sur-
   vival were about 6.1%, being generous.

PART 2

11

I'm not interested in spitting in God's face or shaking the devil by the tail. At the moment I was concerned with Mary Lou, and I have an indefatigable interest in Larry Bancroft. What will become of Larry, I really don't want to know. When I read Rilke's "What will you do God when I die?" I began to admire him above all men. I've always been more concerned with what will become of this world in my absence than with what would become of me after death. Who would weep and carry on, who would love me, who would feed my dogs (I hoped Gloria was doing that now), who would keep track of Orion and the moon and the aggregate beaver exposure in *Playboy*, who would buy the Skippy, my fabled love of peanut butter. I don't any more want to know with certainty what's going to happen to me after I die than I want to know for sure what's going to happen to me tomorrow. If the forecast were good, I might be relieved, but it would spoil the surprise of unlooked-for good fortune. If it were bad, it would spoil everything—like the pleasure of an exquisite roast goose, stuffed with apples and prunes and basted for five hours, being muted by the knowledge that you were to be drawn and quartered before the last mouthful had been massaged through your colon, knowing that it would be more likely delivered caesarean than born anally while reading *The New Yorker*. I pictured the Rosenbergs choking down their fried onions.

The forecast was definitely adverse. I had no desire to be amorphous; and for the sake of my digestion as well as my bones, a change of scenery was in order.

We decided on Santa Fe, mostly because I liked the sound of the name. We packed up the Porsche and headed out at first light. I had a tight pucker string as we passed the city limits and the simultaneous titillation and sweaty palms that always accompany a good escape. I could see William Holden synchronizing his watch in *Stalag 17*; Steve McQueen jumping a barbed wire fence on a stolen motorcycle; and Edmund Dantes, the Count of Monte Cristo, sliding from the walls of the Chateau Def, smiling in his shroud as he fell to freedom in the sea. As for Larry Bancroft, he could see the sun just cresting the mountains in his rear-view mirror as he headed west of 82, half expecting Gunther Henken, his head wrapped in plaster, to step out from the rocks and pull the car to a stop by the sheer force of his massive arms. It brought relief to drop the Porsche down into third gear and test the acceleration. I wanted to leave some kind of trap for him, a sprung custard pie at our apartment door, a Burmese tiger trap filled with cow dung, but decided it was just as well I hadn't. He didn't need any additional exacerbations. I was already afraid he'd pursue me and didn't want to strengthen his motives. I was a fugitive from Gloria, the FBI, and Gunther the Terrible. When I was younger I felt compelled to walk down any street that looked like potential trouble, any dark street teeming with switchblades and whores. I couldn't live with myself if I ever took a detour, and more than once it made for a tense situation, especially during the year I spent in Phoenix, one of the settings of my picaresque education. I arrived at midnight on the train from Chicago, and I took a taxi to the school. I was directed to my dormitory, a stucco building that looked like a leftover from the set of *Fort Apache*. One bare light bulb hung from the ceiling of the common room, casting grotesque shadows on the walls, shadows of switchblades being sharpened, socks being stuffed with rocks, lead pipes, and then *wham* as a chain was tested on the lone table in the center of the room.

"Hi, guys. What's happening?" I asked as casually as I could, trying to imagine how James Dean would have done it. I was even wearing a red nylon windbreaker, exactly like the one he'd worn in *Rebel Without a Cause*.

"We're expecting a raid," said a tall redhead in cowboy shirt. "You Bancroft?" He didn't wait for a reply. "That's your room."

"What kind of a raid?" I asked.

"North Phoenix High," he replied. "What's your weapon?"

I didn't sleep well, but I survived the year and learned switchblade, marijuana, and Bull Durham. I won my letter in calf-roping and bareback bronc-riding. I survived several high-noon encounters in Mesa, Scottsdale, and Phoenix, mostly by being quick and by staying near the edge of the trouble, where I had time to escape when the sheriff arrived. My Venezuelan roommate taught me how to slip out of whorehouses without paying. "You know how to make a hormone? Don't pay her." We made a game of it. If you had to pay, you lost; and whoever lost the most times by the end of the semester was supposed to treat the other to a night with the whore of his choice. But the scoring system wasn't accurate, and I never paid or was treated.

Now I feel no shame in choosing a well-lighted street

or avoiding a bar that looks like trouble. Maybe it's age, maybe I'm just no longer able to suspend my imagination of what might happen to my body, my teeth flying, my lip torn, my nose submerged in my cheek. I've had enough broken bones and distinguishing scars.

I used to watch my shadow on the sidewalk, pleased with the way it looked in my Levi's and denim jacket, particularly in the late afternoon, how long and lean, like the shadow of Wyatt Earp on the streets of Tombstone. I'd stop and admire my shadow while practicing quick draw with a .22 pistol, crouching and firing at the Playmate of the Month tacked to the tree in my father's backyard. I finally gave it up after twice putting a bullet through my leg. You had to be sure to clear the holster before firing.

I was watching my shadow in the square in Santa Fe, depressed by the brilliantly clear sky and the desert scenery. It should have been warmer than it was, a sleepy stucco town full of Indian jewelry and garish desert paintings with brown, brown sand and blue, blue sky. The shadow of a slender monolith in the center of the square intercepted mine, and my eyes followed the path to its base. An old Indian sat on a bench in front of the stone. A grandson of Cochise, I decided. I walked over to the monument and read the inscription:

> THIS MONUMENT DEDICATED
> TO ALL THOSE BRAVE MEN WHO
> LOST THEIR LIVES IN BATTLES
> WITH THE SAVAGE INDIANS IN
> THE EARLY DAYS ON THE
> NEW MEXICO TERRITORY

I started to walk away.
"Do you have a match?"

I turned and saw it was the old chief. "No, I'm sorry. I don't smoke," I said, feeling my pockets.

"There's some nice work down that street," he said, pointing to a row of Indian craft shops with overhanging porches. He didn't talk like Indians I'd seen in the movies.

"Yes, I bet there is," I said, feeling almost guilty about not wanting to look at the jewelry. I wanted to give this man something. I started to walk away again.

"I have some nice girls for you to meet," he said. "Suck, fuck, or like the horses do it."

I was having a bad dream. I went back to the hotel, had a few drinks, and took a nap with Mary Lou.

Perhaps my depression infected Mary Lou or maybe she had her own, those days in a strange place when the sky is hatefully clear, no shelter of clouds, no ceiling to prevent the heat and life from running out and dissipating in space. It's too cold or too hot or too nothing, the wrong time to be, and knowing it will pass doesn't help. The trouble is, it's now, and we made love again and again, joylessly and out of desperation. I remember the story of a man driven to a previously undreamed-of sexual performance by the prospect of violent death. Perhaps I made it up, or maybe it was a fictionalized account of the last days of gladiators, those nights before combat when they were feasted and furnished with perfumed slave girls. My statistics extend into history.

I'm afraid if I knew I was going to die I wouldn't be able to get it up. In any case I don't want to test the theory, not yet anyway. Screw the fried onions; my last meal would be pussy. It isn't actually death I fear, but the manner of dying, the humiliation of a long illness in which you lose control of your functions, the cancer eating you from inside like a hungry rat, and no one will bring you a gun or pills, the violent death that isn't immediate, I'd had a taste of that.

On his way to the guillotine it wasn't thoughts of death that occupied Julien Sorrel but the imagination of his disfigurement. How grotesque his body would appear without a head. After ten years, that was all I could recall of *The Red and the Black*. It hit so close to home. I love my body. It's been with me so long I've come to regard it as my closest friend, the goose pimples on my thigh, sitting in a cold bathroom, my double-jointed thumbs, the lifeline that bisects my left palm, my unusually long toes (I know what you're thinking and it's just an old wives' tale), my orthodontically straightened teeth on which I can play "Yankee Doodle" and "Claire de Lune" with my index finger, my surgically reconstructed nose and chin, the scar of an arrow wound in my right hip from a playmate's father's hunting bow when I was seven, the depression in my ribcage from a football shoe, my rapidly growing fingernails and unmanageable straight blond hair, my red sideburns and the scar above my upper lip where a spring-loaded muscle-builder snapped back in my face, my large chest and tiny wrists, all me, the most familiar territory and body I know. I worry about what will become of it. The thought of it rotting and neglected disgusts me. I've considered taxidermy.

As a child in Florida I fed the porpoises at Marineland and wandered through the fort at St. Augustine, Castile de San Marco. I lingered in the dungeons where Indians died of starvation or suffocated in their own dung. I had a fixation with antiquity and wanted to collect old guns. I wrote Congress to save "Old Ironsides" and still have the newspaper clipping that tells of their decision to do so. The Count of Monte Cristo wasn't a moment's fancy. I lived for months as Edmund Dantes, wronged, exiled, and planning revenge. *The Snow Goose* became an obsession. I read it again and again and cried. I died repeatedly at Dunkirk, only to rise and fly away. Later I became Eugene Gant in my father's endless old house, the drowning brother I never had, drowning again and again, and the stonecutter, an old Dutchman who worked in the garden and stoked the coal furnace. I tagged along imitating his speech and gestures. He told me of Herod, and I saw four men in the furnace when we pulled the clinkers with a long iron rod. I feared my piano teacher, her tantrums and the ruler she used on my knuckles. Before each lesson I soaked my hands in almost scalding water, hoping it would help them make music. In the playworld of dusk on our block, two older girls pulled my pants off, held me down, and massaged my cock—what magic heat, what sorcery made it get hard? I pretended I was undergoing medieval torture, afraid it would break, and I loved it.

We dropped into the warmer lower elevations. Mary Lou slept, and the mesquite began to blend with Saguaro. We were headed for Tucson, where I had a friend. Well, I didn't actually know him, a poet I'd gone to school with. We'd begun corresponding several years before when I read his first book and got his address from Claude Larimer the professor we shared. He was teaching at the University of Arizona, or rather had a sinecure as an assistant to the head of the English Department. He wrote that he hated university life, but it was a living and allowed him time to write. I felt I was going to see an old friend; but at the same time I was afraid he wouldn't like me in person. I'd found in Tom Kalab, for the first time in my own generation, a poet whose poems I wished I'd written, a poet in whom I felt the kinship of Whitman, Neruda, and Appollinaire. I began to get butterflies as we approached Tucson. How should I act? I'll pretend I'm not rich, but of course he'll know. The name "Bancroft" plagues me everywhere. "Just like in the pie," they always say. He liked a few of the poems I sent him, but maybe he'll find me too slick in person. He's probably small and delicate, hypersensitive.

I imagined him blinking a lot and stuttering. I'd be patient and careful about what I said. I hoped he wouldn't be intimidated by Mary Lou. When I really stopped to look at her, she almost intimidated me.

I briefed Mary Lou on what to expect in Tom Kalab. She was excited at the prospect of meeting a real poet, though she wasn't sure why or even what it meant. It was almost dawn when we dropped out of the mountains into Tucson. The valley seemed too flat with the mountains rising all around it, as if it had been excavated. We checked in at a motel on Speedway Boulevard and got some sleep. It was about three o'clock when I called Tom Kalab.

"Sure," he said. "Come on over any time. I'll be here all night. I'm just down the street, as a matter of fact."

We found the stucco house just across from the campus and pulled up at the curb. There was a girl standing in front of the house. She appeared to be shouting, and when I got out of the car I could hear her.

"Goddamn you, Tom Kalab, you motherfucker. You see if you get to use this little twat again." She began pounding on the door. "I'll have you blacklisted all over campus, do you hear me, all over this valley. If you ever want to fuck again, you'd better buy yourself a pig, and a horney one, too."

We stood behind her and waited. There was a long pause, and she seemed to be sobbing. Then she began pounding on the door again, more gently than before. "Tom, please let me in. Please, Tom, you won't be sorry."

The door opened, and a huge man with long red hair done up in a ponytail filled the doorway. "No, goddamnit," he said. "Now get out of my life, will ya?" I looked at Mary Lou, and she gave me that "Oh, my God, what are we doing here?" look. The man in the doorway spotted us. He stuck out his hand and brushed the screaming girl aside. "Larry Bancroft?" he said. "I'm Tom Kalab. Come on in." He seemed to put his arm around both Mary Lou and me and scooped us into the house. He turned and stuck his head out the door and said, "Bye, sweetie."

The pounding resumed, and Kalab said, "Excuse me a minute. I've got to take care of this now, or there'll be a scene." He disappeared down the hall and returned with a galvanized pail filled with water. "Excuse me," he said, and opened the door. The girl was holding her fist in the air, ready to drop it on a door that was no longer there. Kalab took one backswing with the bucket and let the water go. The girl was almost knocked over backward. Her eyes and mouth were wide with shock, and as the water ran off, her T-shirt became transparent.

"You should wear your tits like that more often," said Kalab. "Now take those drowned puppies home." He slammed the door and turned to Mary Lou and me. I was still reeling with surprise, trying to reconcile my image of the poet with the man before me.

"I'm sorry about all that," he said, "but I've got to consider the neighbors. I just can't have that kind of language echoing all over this block."

"Oh, sure," I said. "I know what you mean."

"Nice place you've got here," Mary Lou said, peering into the dark. With the door closed it was hard for me to realize that it was mid-afternoon. The only light in the house came from the black-lighted posters on the walls of the adjoining room and from a single kerosene lamp in the center of a large and low round table. Acid rock came from the room.

"Come on in and meet the family," Kalab said.

When we entered the room, I could see a number of long-haired boys and girls sitting around the table and scattered on chairs and cushions in the corners. The sweet smell of marijuana.

"Hey, everybody, this is Larry Bancroft, a poet from Michigan, and his old lady." He leaned close to Mary Lou and asked, "What's your name?"

"Mary Lou Car . . . I mean, just Mary Lou."

"Larry and Mary Lou," he said. "I won't bother giving you everyone's name. You'll get to know them."

I was glad it was dark, because I blushed when he called me a poet. It was the first time anyone had. I'd just begun trying to focus on the first poet I'd ever met, and now he was calling me a poet, too. Kalab led me to a large overstuffed chair by the table and said, "This is my wife, Penny." A demure face with high cheekbones looked up from the long dark hair around it and asked, "Did you get rid of that dumb cunt?"

"No sweat," said Tom.

I thought the woman in the chair may have been the most classically beautiful woman I'd ever seen. It was dark, like I said; but later, when I saw her in the light of the kitchen, I didn't change my mind. We sat by the table and smoked some grass.

"I hope you'll be able to stay and have some bread with us," Tom said.

"Sure, we'd love to."

Mary Lou still didn't know what to make of it. She was laughing to herself in the dim light of the lamp.

"What brings you to Tucson?" Tom asked.

"Oh, nothing special," I said. "We were just traveling, and I remembered you lived here, so I thought we'd stop by and say hello." I leaned closer to Tom and whispered, "Mary Lou isn't my wife. I kind of just took off a few weeks ago. I met her in a bar in Benton Harbor."

"That's cool. So you're just what, exploring?"

"Yeah, I guess that's what you might call it."

"It can't hurt. Two things a poet needs are travel and romance."

"Yeah, I guess you're right."

There were only four of us for dinner. The boys and girls left, said they were going to some place called Oracle. I asked Tom where they lived, and he said most of them had places of their own but that they "crashed" here sometimes and all chipped in with money and housework. We had some wine with our soup and homemade bread, and the kitchen took on a soft glow. I felt as if I'd known Tom and Penny a long time. I think Mary Lou was still a little ill at ease, probably because Tom and I were talking about poets and poetry, which was a foreign language to her. Tom said that Jim Harrison had just read at the University and that Gary Snyder was coming next month.

"Did Robert Frost ever read here?" Mary Lou asked. I think Robert Frost was the only poet's name she could think of.

"Yes, he did as a matter of fact," Tom said. "He was the first poet to read here when they opened up the poetry center." Mary Lou seemed pleased to have gotten that in.

"Hey, maybe it's none of my business," I said, "but what was all that about with the girl in front of the house?"

"It seems to be everybody's business," Penny said. "She's just one of the little tarts that follow Tom around. She lived here for awhile, but she decided she wanted to make it permanent, I mean she and Orpheus here. He sluiced her pond once or twice, and she decided she wanted him to swim in it forever. She wasn't much," she said, scooping up her long hair and pressing it to the top of her head.

"You didn't mind?" I asked, afraid I was again overstepping. "I mean that he 'sluiced her pond'?"

"No, he needs that for his ego," she said, "and it makes him a lot easier to live with." Tom's face seemed flushed. He was smiling in his wine. "It's all right as long as they don't get possessive."

"Gee, that's nice," said Mary Lou. "I bet there'd be a lot fewer broken homes if they weren't all locked up so tight."

Tom put on a Rod Stewart record, and we went back to the big table and lit up.

I wondered how Gloria would have reacted if she had been there. She might have just clammed up and told me later that she "didn't wish to see those people again." She probably would have been hurt "to think that people could live that way." Gloria had the enviable ability to shut out anything she didn't like, obliterate it, forget it, gone. "I don't want to believe people do that," she'd always say, and after that she didn't. She seemed eminently sane. I don't think I ever knew anyone saner than Gloria, in fact she was so goddamn sane it drove me crazy. It was kind of like being married to your mother, not your real mother but your ideal mother. Taking a shower, I'd sometimes fall in love with the graceful blonde on the shampoo bottle. She was so serene and delicate, so remote and pristine that I wanted to stick my cock in all that gorgeous long hair. There was always something sensuous in her upper lip. I'd get so charged up that I'd have to turn away from the shower head, or the water beating down on the one-eyed trouser lord was more than I could bear. I'd towel off quickly and go take it out on Gloria. She'd protest at first, but in the end she loved it. In fact the only time I think she enjoyed making love was when I half raped her. Several times she asked me to tie her wrists and ankles to the bed frame, but that was too kinky, even for me. Now I'd do it at the slightest suggestion, but at the time, as I said, she was my ideal mother. The fantasy of making love to your mother when she was twenty-five or thirty, of being back in the womb when it was young and tight, now that you could really appreciate it, with a man's knowledge and a child's eye. *Oh never can we recapture that first fine careless rapture, the glory in the flower, the splendor in the grass. The child is father of the man, and so it must always be, tied each to each in natural piety.* But in the fantasy, it was the ideal mother, the older woman, who seduced you, not the other way around. I always maintained my innocence, the lamb led to the slaughter. I almost lived it out with a whore in London when I was seventeen, a redhead about thirty. "Would you like to come home with me, three pounds, around the corner?" she said. Tea and sympathy, but the tea wasn't free, and the "three pounds, around the corner" gave it a distinctly sour flavor.

When I was dating Gloria she wasn't the mother, she was the golden virgin who, when the right chords were sounded, became the goddess of love. She was free and romantic and inventive about it, a lot like Mary Lou, as a matter of fact. But when the children came, our children, she became my mother as well as theirs. I was on the outside looking in, my nose pressed to the glass of the pastry shop, the oldest child thrown over for the new baby, all squiggly and wrapped in powder. Then the moral edicts began and all the paperback books by Haim Ginott and Dr. Spock. She told me how to behave with the children and finally how to behave with her.

> *I slunk around the she-bear's den*
> *hoping to get in again*
> *but now the den was occupied*
> *and I must seek warmth in my own sweet hide.*

I left the rhyme on her pillow, but she didn't say a word about it. Later she told me to "stop being such a big baby." I wonder about monogamy and marriage contracts. I think they give a woman exactly what she wants and at the same time spoil it for her. The romance is gone. I still wanted to send her candy and flowers, but she always gave the candy to the kids and put the flowers on the dining room table on the way to her bridge party with an "Oh, isn't that nice." Maybe that's why married men are more frequently unfaithful than are married women, getting back to statistics. It's not so much lust as the need for romance. Women grow up and get over it, but men never do. I never did, and when I got to the end of my cord, Gloria would always reel me in and set me straight. "Yes, mother, you're right as usual," and I'd carry out the garbage and fix the lawn mower; and once or twice a week, she'd surrender her body to me, close her eyes, and wait till I was through. I always felt I should leave some money on the pillow to compensate for my gross display of carnal appetites. I thought of the whore in London. Maybe three pounds wasn't such a bad price after all. It was honest work, and I might have learned something. As it was, I told her I had a "season ticket," the only casual way I could think of to get out of it, and it had sounded so friendly: "Won't you come home with me?" like Eliza Doolittle, not "Do ya wanna screw?" Seventeen and all alone in London. I almost ran after her to beg her to take me home with her, but something wouldn't let me, and I've been sorry for that something ever since.

As I held the smoke deep in my lungs and passed the joint to Penny, I tried to imagine how she really felt about Tom screwing college girls in the next room. I mean, shitting on your own doorstep is one thing, but shitting in your own house, even if you have permission to. What, I wondered, did they say to each other when he walked out of the spare bedroom, pulling up his pants and the girl still lying there, coming down off it. "Feel better, darling?" or "Was she any good?" Maybe she just told him to carry out the garbage, maybe it really wasn't so different. Could she hear the sounds through the wall, the bed squeaking, the moans and cries, the heavy breathing, the laughter? I watched her pulling on the joint. She was so quiet it was scary, so intimidatingly demure, I felt I was a little in love with her.

Now Tom had the joint, and it glowed under his dark red moustache. What a mistake it was to try to equate a man's life with his work, to try to know the artist from his biography, and thinking you knew him well, to turn to his work and find it the work of a stranger. Maybe it wasn't always true. Shakespeare was so many things. Kindly old grandfather Frost was a real son of a bitch, "Une Saison En Enfer" was hardly the product of a nineteen-year-old mind, and wizened, crazy Ezra Pound practically a saint. Thomas Kalab, the pure, sensitive, almost delicate poet was as Rabelaisian as any man I'd met or imagined, tender only to the Muse.

And now Mary Lou had the joint, sweet, sexy Mary

Lou. Was she so different from Gloria at that age, was she? Mary Lou, not knowing where we were going, escaping a trapped life, just like me. Trusting Mary Lou. I hardly knew her, and she'd put her future in my hands. "Wherever you wanna go Larry, *that's* where I want to go." I wondered if I was the father she'd never had (her parents divorced when she was six), sweet, beautiful Mary Lou, not a rough spot on her. I pulled on the joint and watched Mary Lou through the glow just beyond my nose, her head back, her eyes on the ceiling, and her beautiful teeth, her beautiful teeth. The smoke was deep in my lungs, and James Taylor was singing "Fire and Rain." Beautiful Mary Lou.

13

My father wanted to be a railroad man, an engineer. "It's in my blood," he told me one day in his basement railroad room. He didn't keep his room a secret, but there were few people who actually saw it. "Happiness is wanting what you have, not having what you want," he said. He wanted to be an engineer, back when being an engineer really meant something, back in the days of steam. "If I'd gone into railroads, the railroads wouldn't have failed," he said. "It was steam that kept this country running, steam. When diesels came along the engineers lost interest, and so did everyone else. Trains just became another way to get somewhere. Even the service in the dining cars fell off, and the porters got lazy. Why, I remember the first time your grandfather and I took the limited. . . ."

My father's railroad room had layers and layers of tracks, one over the other, suspended on bridges, mountains, overpasses, underpasses, tracks intersecting at all angles and levels, and a control room with a glass partition separating him from his trains. A control panel against the glass wall looked like the cockpit of a 747, an incomprehensible field of switches, flashing lights, electric timers; and the table below it was covered with loose-leaf notebooks, freight charts, timetables, slide rules, and an IBM calculating machine. He worked constantly to make his trains more efficient, to make them safer, and to cut down station time. It was his evening world, his world of might-have-been. Of course he'd never admit that he ever seriously considered becoming an engineer. There was Bancroft Industries, canned peas at that time, the First World War, and a job waiting for him when he came back from France—never any question about what he'd do. "In those days you did what had to be done. There wasn't all this confusion and unhappiness of too much freedom of choice. I'll tell you, in a lot of ways I think I was lucky." Though he was forty-four years old when I was born, and in my earliest memories he must have been fifty, I always thought of him as nineteen. I had a faded brown photograph of him in his sergeant's uniform, and that's how I always thought of him. He was a contemporary. I'd heard his story of Château-Thierry and Alsace-Lorraine so many times that my first thoughts of him were always as the sergeant, the scout. I never grew tired of hearing them. He told of the French girl he'd found bayoneted by the Germans, the days and nights without food or sleep, the artillery barrage, the dumplings that made him sick when he finally got back behind Allied lines, the troop ship he'd missed on a Friday the thirteenth that had been torpedoed with no survivors, and finally of coming home and wondering what it had all been for.

I woke up before dawn and lay listening to a train whistle somewhere beyond the window. It was a sound I hadn't heard for a long time, an almost hypnotic sound. How many great movies begin with a train pulling into town, bringing a stranger or "the new marshall." I thought of a story by Willa Cather in which everyone was waiting at the depot for a train, bringing the body of an artist, a famous sculptor, back to the town where he was born, back to all the insensitive people who'd threatened to destroy him and had driven him away in the first place, and *Picnic*, with a train whistle and William Holden standing between freight cars through a veil of steam, destined to love Kim Novak. I hadn't heard a whistle like that since I used to play hobo every Saturday, packing a Spam sandwich in my knapsack and cutting over fields to lie on my belly on a grass bank and wait for the train, always dreaming of jumping it, dreaming of where we would go. When it finally came, I'd duck from the shower of sparks as the engine passed and watch the freight cars flash by in a stream of exotic names: Lackawanna, Erie, Great Northern, Southern, Illinois, Route of the Phoebe Snow, C&O, flatcars, boxcars, tankers, coal cars, and finally a red caboose. The whistle grew fainter, and I strained in the dark to hear it as long as I could. I wasn't sure I could hear it anymore. Maybe I was making that faint moan in my head. I heard a few birds singing early and now and then the *whir* of tires on the boulevard.

I was the same age my father would have been in 1929, the depression setting in and the canning plant operating on half shifts, but "people still had to eat, you know." He'd been through a war, come home with the Croix de Guerre and gone right back to work, hero for a day. He was given an honorary high school diploma in 1958, the same year I was supposed to graduate, though I couldn't march in the ceremony. It was kind of awkward, I guess; what would they say? "We were going to have a father and son receiving their diplomas together today, but unfortunately, the son's in jail." I imagine they skipped that part of it, at least I hope they did. My father never talked about it.

I got out of bed and watched the streaks of sunlight shooting up over the mountains. Tom was picking us up at nine to take us to the Sonora Desert Museum and then out to Oracle, an art colony in the mountains to the north, for dinner. Everyone called it "the ranch." I looked at Mary Lou, and she was stretching, arching her back, her arms over her head and her toes pointed, in the best traditions of modern dance. "Hey, you, come 'ere," she said, half yawning. She always felt sexy in the morning, which usually meant I did too. I walked over to the bed. She put her hand on my knee and ran it slowly up the inside of my thigh, finally cradling my balls. I stood by the bed, silently enjoying it. She reached up with both hands, pulled down my shorts and kissed me softly around the base of my cock. She took my cock in her hand and kissed up and down the shaft. I looked at the part in her hair and across the room where I could see us in the mirror. I looked back down at Mary Lou, and I felt I was floating somewhere up around the ceiling, bumping it like a newly released helium balloon. She put her hand in the small of my back and pulled me down, her long hair flowing down to me and her breasts falling away from her body. We were still in bed when I heard Tom knocking. "Hey, anybody alive in there? I know what you're doing," he shouted. I opened the door.

"Come on in."

Mary Lou wrapped herself in a sheet and walked into the bathroom, bouncing on the balls of her feet. "Hi, Tom," she said, and closed the door.

"I wasn't wrong, was I?"

"How could you tell?"

"You've got that smile on your face, and I imagined what I'd be doing in here if I were you."

"I never have a choice," I said. "I'm just a prisoner of love."

We had breakfast in the motel coffee shop, and the eggs were cold. Tom asked to see the manager, and a man about forty-five with a 1950s crewcut and a blue blazer walked perfunctorily to our table.

"I'm Tom Kalab, and these are my friends, Larry Bancroft and Mary Lou."

"How do you do," said the manager, holding out his right hand. I think he was going to tell us his name, but before he got it out, Tom laid a fried egg across his palm. The manager stopped in midsentence. He looked down at his hand, at the quivering white and yolk running through his fingers with eyes almost larger than his horn-rimmed glasses.

"You feel that?" said Tom. "That's cold."

"So it is," the manager said. "So it is." He stared at the amorphous mess in his hand.

"Well, I'm showing my friends here Tucson, and this isn't any way to start 'em off. I don't want 'em to think this is the way we eat out here." He affected the drawl perfectly. The same drawl every doctor's son from Scarsdale affects when he starts hanging out around horses, with the long O's in on. He called himself Tome.

"No, well, I see what you mean," said the manager. "Well, I'm awfully sorry this happened, and I'm going to ask the cook to make you another nice *hot* breakfast right now. You've got no idea how hard it is to find good help. No idea. And there'll be no charge for this breakfast, no charge." He was cradling the egg in both hands now as he hurried toward the kitchen.

"It usually works," Tom said, picking his teeth.

14

Tom had the courage or the gall to do all the things I only imagined. I could always handle physical situations, that is, situations that demanded physical courage. It wasn't too hard to choke down visions of death and dismemberment and plow into something potentially dangerous; but to risk mortification, that took social courage, and that I didn't have. I was always intimidated by waiters and sales clerks, especially in New York. I was intimidated by everyone in New York, even hotel maids. I never knew what to say when I'd return to my room and find the maid there. "Hi, mind if I come in? Say, you do nice work. Well, I can see you're busy. I'll come back later." I remember doing laps around the Palm Court at the Plaza when I had to take a dump, and the maid was in my room. I always shied away from public toilets. I believed those stories of V.D. and toilet seats, the anal conditioning of my youth. Anyway, I did laps till the urge passed; but then I ended up getting constipated and took Ex-lax, which worked too well, and spent days chained to my room, with the chain on the door to keep the maid out.

I used to get constipated a lot when I was a kid. We had a Baptist babysitter who told my sister and me stories about the judgment day and the fires of hell, lakes of fire to which we are destined. My parents were casual Christians, and she knew it; Congregationalists, in fact, about as casual as you can get. My sister was older and turned all this her way by threatening to flush me down the toilet if I didn't do as she wished. She said she'd just pull that chain and whoosh, flush me into the lake of fire. I avoided the bathroom for days. She made me give her half my allowance, made me play dolls, and several times when we were home alone, she dressed me in her white pinafore, threw me out in the street, and locked the door. I soon became the best fighter on the block. What I lacked in muscle I made up in fury. They called me the "madwoman of Dayton Street," but never to my face, never more than once.

Tom moved in his own atmosphere. Nothing seemed to penetrate. He filled the room with his ambience, and no matter how many people there were, Tom was the only one you were aware of. Everything generated from and around him. He was the sun of whatever solar system he entered. He didn't seem to work at it; he was just Tom, Tom the center, a law of nature. Everything at Oracle seemed to stop when we arrived. We entered Bruce McGregor's house in the middle of a party. Everything stopped. It seemed rehearsed, like a Howard Keel entrance in one of those musical shows where all the girls are dressed in gingham and the boys in blue jeans and checkered shirts and you really can't tell them apart. Tom walked in and stood by the door, and the party gravitated to him. He received his homage so gracefully that he probably wasn't even aware it was happening, as if he were a king, and this was just a way of life.

Bruce McGregor was larger than Tom and wore a green plaid kilt and a beautiful red beard. His house was red Victorian, plush red Victorian like a cartoon scheme of a nineteenth-century whorehouse. Red Victorian chairs, red wallpaper, red rugs on the polished hardwood floor, gold framed mirrors, and a red runner up the stairs. Bruce gave me a drink and said, "So you're the poet from Michigan?" In Tucson I was famous. I decided to accept it gracefully. Tom was holding court, Mary Lou was holding my arm, and Bruce proceeded to show us around. We stepped out the front door, and the full moon outlined the mountains and the saguaro. There were a number of buildings scattered in the hills. Bruce waved his arm in a semicircle and said, "This is the ranch." He said that most of the houses belonged to people from the art department. He told us they'd gotten together, bought an abandoned ranch, and moved on some old houses that had lain in the path of the new highway. They'd built a common studio with skylights, kilns, and potting rooms and held many of their classes out there. I asked Bruce about his kilt, and he said he belonged to the Highland Marching Band, played the base drum, but that he liked the kilt so well that he wore it most of the time. "I never wear it in dust storms, though," he said. "It's hard on me tool." I didn't bother to ask if he wore anything under it, because just then he decided to "take a wee" from the front porch. He lifted his kilt and let go.

It felt good to get back in the warmth of the house, and I had just gotten inside the door when someone handed me a joint. The someone told me she was Polly Boland. I took a deep pull and decided that, from now on, I would consider myself a poet. Bruce swept Mary Lou into the kitchen, and Polly Boland said she'd heard a lot about me.

"Really?" I said. I thought my "really" sounded a lot like Terry-Thomas.

"I heard you were quite a stud back in Michigan."

"Really?" I said again. Now I was feeling really silly. She passed me the joint again, and I took another deep pull and held the smoke in my lungs.

"That's what they say," she said, resting her arm on the door jamb and leaning toward me.

"Really?"

"Is that all you can say?" she demanded.

"No. Actually I can say quite a few things." I still sounded like Terry-Thomas.

"Like what?"

"Like I haven't heard a thing about you, but I bet you're quite a stud, too." Somehow that wasn't quite what I meant. "Hey, that rhymes," I said, trying to take the onus off it.

"Look, beefcake, are you insinuating . . .?"

"No. I'm not insinuating anything. I just meant that I thought you would be very nice, er, are very nice." Polly wasn't really what you'd call beautiful. Polly was what you'd call "tough" when you used it as a term of appreciation, sort of like the "teen angel" who raped me in all my adolescent dreams.

"Well, okay," she said, "but just watch how you say it. Take this." She handed me something that looked like a cold capsule.

"What is it?" I asked, holding it up to the light.

"What do you care? It's good for you."

"Okay," I said, and washed it down with gin or vodka or whatever I was drinking.

"I like your poems," Polly said.

"You do? Where have you seen them?"

"Tom showed 'em to me. I like the one about the pine-apple best, but the one about the girl in the barber shop's real tender."

"Are you a student?" I asked. It was the first real attention I'd gotten since I decided to consider myself a poet, and I didn't know quite how to handle it.

"I just got my M.A., but I haven't decided whether I'll go on."

"Really?" I said, quite amazed.

"Now cut that shit out. I warned you once."

"I'm sorry." The room began to go flimsy, like silly putty, and the noises of the party poured in on me like a waterfall.

"I-I-I- fe-e-el stra-a-ange," I said, my voice echoing. Kris Kristofferson was singing, "Silver Tongued Devil," and I imagined I was looking at his tonsils. "I don't feel very silver-tongued," I echoed at Polly. She was all I could see clearly.

"Come on, baby beef, I know what you need." She put her hands on my ribs and pulled me toward the stairs. They seemed endless but effortless, up, up, up. The noise of the party was fading, a little meadow stream, gurgling over the rocks far below.

15

The sun hit me like an anvil. It came through the window as if someone had turned on an arc light. I recoiled and covered my eyes. I peeked through my fingers at the high ceiling. There was a large crack running all the way across it. I decided it looked like the back of a triceratops, then changed my mind in favor of a giraffe's neck. Finally it just looked like a crack in the plaster. The room had those high casement windows I'd seen in farmhouses in Michigan. There was a painting on the wall above the dresser where the mirror should have been. It was a picture of a naked girl chasing a motorcycle. Of course. I wondered where I was and then decided that was too corny a thing to wonder. In how many movies does James Bond or Michael Caine or Dana Andrews or Humphrey Bogart wake up and say, "Where am I?" No, my sense of decorum wouldn't allow it. "Where do I happen to be?" was better. So I sat up and asked myself, "Where do I happen to be?" I'm not on my Aunt Hilda's farm because Aunt Hilda never cared for pictures of naked ladies chasing motorcycles. I'm not even on a farm because I don't hear any animals. I'm not in my own little bed at home because I don't recognize the crack in the ceiling. I'm not even in

Michigan because those lumps outside the window appear to be cacti. I must be in Arizona or . . . Yes, I'm in Arizona. I was in Tucson. I saw a coral snake at the Desert Museum, but I don't think it was real. I watched him for an hour in his glass case, but he never moved. They could have easily put a rubber snake in there. It would have been a lot easier than going to all the trouble of catching a real coral snake. It's a fraud. Maybe other animals, the ones that did move, were animated by Disney, even the otter that Mary Lou fell in love with. Oh yes, Mary Lou. I was in Arizona with Mary Lou. We watched the otter at the Desert Museum, and Mary Lou decided she wanted an otter for her very own. I offered to get her a jaguar, but she insisted on an otter. Tom Kalab was standing next to Mary Lou. That's it, we went to the Desert Museum with Tom Kalab, and then we were going to a party at Oracle, at the ranch. Bruce McGregor's kilt. That's where I am, at the ranch. But why did I spend the night here? Polly, Polly, Polly Boland, my teen angel. If anything happened it was a waste. She told me she liked my poems. That's nice. But after that . . . What's the use of anything if you can't remember it. I sniffed the sheets for a trace of Polly, but all I could smell was me. Then on the pillow a trace of perfume, but maybe that was there before. I was in Bruce McGregor's house, but whose bed was I sleeping in? I pulled on my Levi's, picked up my shirt and boots, and felt my way through the hall and down the stairs. When I got to the bottom I could see Bruce McGregor, wrapped in a white apron, breaking eggs into a large bowl. "Ahemmm," I coughed, not knowing how to begin. Bruce tilted his head back and looked at me through his chin whiskers. "Ah, good morning, laddie-buck. Did you sleep well?"

"I don't know. I don't even remember being awake."

"Oh, you were awake, all right. You were awake at one time."

"This isn't a scene from *Brigadoon*, is it?" I asked.

"What's that you say?"

"Oh, nothing. What did I do when I was awake?"

"Well, you went upstairs with Polly Boland, but what happened after that only Polly knows, and she left long ago."

"I went upstairs with Polly Boland. Is that really her name?"

"Nobody knows that either, but it's good enough, and it fits her. That's a famous trick she has, you know."

"A famous trick?"

Bruce poured the eggs in a large skillet. "Yes, indeed, a famous trick. Did she give you a pill?"

"Well, yeah, now that I think of it, she did. What was it?"

"Nobody knows but Polly."

"That would make a good song title."

"What's that?"

"Nobody knows but Polly."

"Don't think it hasn't been thought of before. Yes, indeed, a famous trick."

"What's all this trick shit? What's the point of the trick?"

"Well, Polly says her pill does two things. It makes 'em last longer, and they can't talk afterward 'cause they don't remember what happened."

"That's kind of selfish of her, isn't it?"

Bruce flipped a large omelet from the pan onto a platter. "Well, selfish it may be, but that's her way. Polly's a 'right now' girl. Sit down." Bruce put half the omelet on my plate and brought me a mug of coffee. He hung his apron on a mannequin that looked like Rudy Vallee and sat down across the table.

"She might have corrupted me."

"Well, if she did you don't remember it, and if you don't have any corrupt memories, you can't really have been corrupted."

I could see that he was obviously right. "Well this is awfully nice of you," I said. "And I appreciate you putting me up for the night."

"Oh, no trouble at all. It happens frequently, and a poet is always welcome here."

Ah, yes, the poet, I thought. So this is what it's like being a poet. When I just wrote poems, things were pretty dull; but being a poet is a whole new world. How long can this go on? Then I remembered Mary Lou. I asked Bruce about Mary Lou, and he said that Tom had taken her home sometime after I disappeared with Polly. Tom took her home? Did that mean he took her to his home or back to the motel? Did he just give a ride or did he *take her home?* I didn't ask Bruce. I wasn't in any position to be indignant.

I thanked Bruce for the breakfast and the bed and hitch-hiked back to Tucson. I got a ride with an old cowboy in a 1952 Ford pickup. The truck was rusty, and the cowboy didn't say a word. He just kept rolling and smoking Bull Durham cigarettes, one after the other. I tried conversation several times. I thought I at least owed it to him to be sociable. "Nice truck you've got here. It's a '52, isn't it?" He didn't even nod. He let me off on Speedway, near Tom's house. I said, "Thanks for the ride," and he drove off like a Walter Brennan robot. I walked by Tom's house on the far side of the street. I decided not to stop. I wouldn't know what to say. I could thank him for taking Mary Lou home and then ask him where she was. If she was there, I didn't want to find her. If he was with her at the motel, that was a more dramatic place to discover them. I got madder and madder as I got closer to the motel. I began to rehearse all the hurt, indignant things I was going to say. "My girl and the best friend I have in Tucson, maybe even in the world, ha!"

I think blue is the most erotic color. When I imagine a woman all heated up, I imagine her turning slightly blue or purple like a pale grape, the blue of a vein just blushing through the skin of the breast. That's what I saw when Mary Lou opened the door. She was wearing a cotton floor-length nightie, the top three buttons undone, and there was that pale blue vein running into her left breast. The sunlight was streaming into the room from behind me, and Mary Lou was squinting, still full of sleep. I looked at her cleavage and the vein in her left breast.

"Boy, you make a lot of noise," she said. "What do you want?" My fist hurt from pounding on the door.

"What do I want?" I said in disbelief. "What do I want?"

"That's what I said. What do you want?"

"Well, I'm here."

"Oh?"

"Yes, I'm here, and I want to know what you have to say for yourself?"

"What I have to say for myself? I can't believe this. What did you have in mind?"

"Well, you can begin by explaining about you and Tom."

"Me and Tom? What about me and Tom?"

"Well, I know he brought you home. Are you alone?"

"No, I'm shacked up here with Molly O'Toole, or whatever that little tart's name is." She sounded a lot like Gloria, I thought. "Of course I'm alone."

I walked into the room and couldn't see anyone. "Why

did you go home with Tom? Why did you leave me?" I was genuinely hurt.

"What was I supposed to do, crawl in between you and that mink you were with?"

I hadn't thought of that. "Oh." I was stumped for a moment. "Is that what happened?"

"You know damned well that happened, and so did everyone at the party. I was never so humiliated in my life. Really, Larry, there I was, along with everyone else, watching you pole-vault up the stairs with that person." She began to cry.

I hadn't thought of it that way. My anger was gone, and I began to shrink like a beach ball with a hole in it. At least I was in the room, and we were alone. "Would you believe me if I said that I didn't know what I was doing?"

"Does a salmon know what it's doing when it swims up-river to spawn?"

"Look, Mary Lou, I don't even know if anything happened. She slipped me a pill."

"Oh, that's rich. Are you trying to tell me you were raped?"

"Well, I hadn't considered that word, but now that you mention it, maybe I was raped. I don't remember a thing after we went upstairs." I still don't think she believed me, but she began to calm down. My whole day had been turned upside down. I was all worked up to be the injured party and ended up as the louse, the one time I really hadn't been a louse, I don't think. I asked her what Tom said about the whole thing.

"He said he could understand why I was upset, but that Molly what's-her-name did that sort of thing all the time and that you weren't anything special."

I resented the way she phrased that. I think I was forgiven, but she made me see a doctor and get a blood test as a precaution against Polly's varied past. The test was premature and negative. After a few minutes of conversation about how I was changing, she let it go. She said she wanted to call her mother in Benton Harbor. They weren't really very close, but she wanted to talk to her; she said she'd be worried about her disappearance. It had been a couple of weeks.

I didn't know where to begin with Tom. I was embarrassed about all the things I'd imagined. Then I realized that Tom didn't know I'd imagined them. I felt better. Mary Lou said that her mother was all right, but that her disappearance had caused a lot of talk among her friends. She never had approved of her job at the Silver Cloud.

We drove over to Tom's house, but he wasn't there. Penny said that he'd gone to the office and asked us to come back about dinner time. That sounded kind of funny, Tom "gone to the office." I wasn't going to the office anymore, but Tom was. Penny suggested we take a drive up Mount Lemmon and told us how to get started.

We didn't talk much on the drive up. The road was twisty, switchbacking up the mountain, and the Porsche was in its element. I was busy shifting and turning, and Mary Lou was watching the valley grow small below us. I thought about Gloria on the way up. Sooner or later I had to think about what I was going to do and when I was going to do it. I wondered if everything was all right at home and then reflected that that sounded awfully provincial, considering the life I'd had in the last two weeks. Maybe they thought I was dead; maybe they'd had me declared insane. Of course the police would be looking for me, but they'd have no idea where to begin. Lots of people disappear. What was Gloria planning, what revenge? She couldn't have just forgotten about me. Maybe she'd taken a lover, but who? In Brainard? She was too circumspect for that. Maybe she'd gone to New York; maybe she'd gone to San Francisco. Maybe I'd run into her there, and we'd have a drink and talk about what a small world it was. How would I introduce Mary Lou? How would I introduce Gloria? What would Gloria and Mary Lou have to say to each other? Maybe everybody'd just forgotten about me. Maybe Gloria'd written it off to my being a little crazy. I never lived up to her expectations, never "cultivated the right friends." I never played golf either, and that irked her. "Everybody plays golf. How are you really going to get to know anyone if you don't play golf?" Gloria played golf and knew "everyone" at the club. I drank beer and knew "everyone" at the Pine Tar Tavern. I knew Ben Flatt who ran the gas station, and Sam Carter, the game warden, and Joe what's-his-name, Italian something-or-other—I don't know what he does—but he shoots a good game of pool. I knew all those people who played golf, too, knew them from the office, and forty hours a week was enough. I knew a lot of other people, too, but I didn't know their names. I knew their problems and their faces and the way they talked. They'd all wonder where I was. "Good for him," they'd say. "Good for him." Or maybe they wouldn't. I don't know. And who is the girl sitting next to me, barely known her two weeks, barely know more than her name and the way she makes love, just beginning to know that, it's always a surprise, I'll say that for her, only two weeks and it feels like it's been ten years, as comfortable as that and as irritating, two weeks I've led my own life, done as I please, and is it any better than when it wasn't mine? Yes, but disappointingly so. Tomorrow looks like a vacuum, just there to be sucked up and on to another, and how many loves have I judged from my own? The girl I went with in high school ended up getting fat, divorced, working in a bar in Cleveland, and I pitied her, pity her, a failure, a miserable failure, her life at a dead end? I thought so, how many like that, but maybe she didn't, hadn't considered that, maybe it's what she always wanted and didn't know it. Maybe she's happier than she's ever been. "Better a man should do what he wants and fail than be a successful nobody," Miller said; and I am doing what I want, obviously for the moment, but a man can't spend his life in a car just dropping in, Buzz and Todd, just watching for a few days and moving on. If I went back to Brainard, would it be any different, could I make it any different? If only I had a script to follow I could play the part with ease, but I've played the script all my life. I'd play the script in Brainard; every week begins on Monday and ends on Friday, and on the weekends there's golf to be played or avoided, simple as that, but here's the top of the mountain, only snow back home.

We got out of the car and walked out on the rock ledge. We hadn't said a word all the way up. It didn't seem strange, but it occurred to me when we walked in the cold air. We could see the whole valley below us.

"It's some view," Mary Lou said. It wasn't much of a comment, wasn't very perceptive, a simple "oh" would have done it.

It looked like one of the landscapes in my father's train room. I told Mary Lou about my father's trains and that I'd heard the whistle from what sounded like a steam engine, the first one I'd heard in years. It was late afternoon, and a ridge of red light was beginning to form above the mountains to our left. It reminded me of a Gene Autry movie, and I mentioned it to Mary Lou, but she said she'd never seen a Gene Autry movie. I was a little shocked by that and reflected on how much difference there must have been in the heroes we grew up with, almost ten years. She was born after the Korean War and wouldn't remember radio either, real radio, "The Shadow" and "Just Plain Bill" and "Suspense" and "Kindly Old Dr. Christian." I was jacking off before she was even born.

"Let's go back to the car," I said. I was cold, and all that scenery was beginning to depress me. I love an ordinary sunset in Michigan, but spectacular scenery depresses me. My parents took me to Lake Louise when I was eleven and got me up to see the famous sunrise. It was beautiful, but it depressed me. We took the train, of course, the C&O, The Milwaukee Road, The Canadian Pacific. My father timed every leg with a stopwatch, and I went horseback riding with a girl from La Crosse, Wisconsin, and fell in love. She was three years older, but she was friendly, and on the trip home the train stopped in La Crosse. It was early morning and I looked out the window from my sleeper berth and saw the sign that said La Crosse. I thought of her. I wondered if she still thought of me. La Crosse looked like a lonely place. I wondered if she was happy there.

It felt good to get out of the wind, and I started the car and turned the heater up full. It seemed especially cold to be cold in Arizona.

"We'd better get going if we're going to Kalab's for dinner," Mary Lou said. I thought about her and Tom and the things I'd imagined. She seemed pretty anxious to get there, and I told her so.

"I'm not anxious, I'm hungry," she said, "and I've got the good manners to want to be on time."

"Oh, now it's my manners, is it?"

"I didn't say anything about your manners. I was talking about my manners."

"No, but you implied . . ."

"I didn't imply anything. You implied that I was especially anxious to see Tom."

"I never mentioned Tom; I said 'Kalab's.' You're the one who brought up Tom, which proves you're the one who was thinking about him."

"Larry, why are you starting this again? Let's remember who left who last night."

"Whom."

"What do you mean, whom?"

"It's who left whom, not who left who."

"Look, will you cut that shit out. You know what I meant, and you're just doing that to torment me." She started crying silently and took out a Kleenex and blew her nose. She always won when she cried.

"Okay, I'm sorry. I've been a little on edge, and I guess I've been letting it show. I got used last night, too. Don't forget that."

"Oh, come on, Larry."

"Okay, okay, if you don't want to believe me." I leaned over and took her head in my hands and kissed her on the forehead. I put the car in gear, released the parking brake, and we started rolling down the mountain. "I wuve you," I said.

"I know. It's all that keeps me going."

"Knock, knock," I said.

"Oh, Jesus, Larry."

"Oh, come on. Knock, knock."

"Who's there?" she said with a sigh.

"Fuck."

"Fuck who?"

"Fuck whom."

"That's so old," she said, laughing.

"Then why are you laughing?"

"Because it's so old," she said, still laughing.

We stopped for gas on the way back to Tucson. There was a horse trailer parked by the side of the station, and the man who came out to the pumps wore a high-crown straw cowboy hat. He must have been about fifty, and his belly hung over his jeweled silver belt-buckle. I'd seen that trick before. You could buy trousers four inches smaller if you wore them below your belly instead of around it. His black boots were "real shiny" and had tooled silver tips on the toes that matched his belt. "He weren't no ordinary cowboy."

"Howdy," he said. "This little car use real gasoline?"

"Shore does," I said in my best drawl. "You damn betcha."

"Hey, watch your language," he said a little righteously.

"Sorry," I said.

"I hear so much of that crude kind of talk it's difficult not to pick it up. But I watch it real close. I always like to think the Lord's helping me run this station, and I don't want nothing said he wouldn't want to hear."

"Cheap help."

"What's that you say?" he said, squinting at me.

"I say it shore helps. To have the Lord around, I mean."

"I could tell right off you's a straight sort of feller," he said.

"Could I have some gas, please?"

"Yup. Shore can." It sounded like he was imitating me. "Fill 'er up?"

"Yup," I said.

I pulled the knob that released the gas cap cover on the front fender.

"Is that where you put the gas in?"

"Yup," I said.

"Well, I'll be cow-kicked in a mud puddle," he said. "Ain't that cute. Check your oil?" he asked, walking around to the front of the car.

"It ain't there, and it's all right," I hollered.

He backed away and looked at the license plate. "Well, I'll be. You folks is from Michigan. I'm from Michigan myself. What town you from?"

"Brainard," I said.

"Never heard of it." he said. "I'm from Hamtramck myself, but I come out here for the horses and the sunshine. Been out here about a year now."

"Well, I'll be cow-kicked," I said. "It shows." Mary Lou started to giggle.

"The show? You folks out here for the horse show? I bet you are. I can just tell horse people right off."

"The whatness of horseness is allhorse," I said.

"Ain't that the truth," he said. "Ain't that just the truth."

16

A letter from Gloria. When we got to Kalab's, Penny handed me a letter from Gloria. The letter had been forwarded from Aspen, addressed to me in care of Ozzie Pierce, then forwarded in care of Tom Kalab at the University. She wanted to know why, that was the gist of it; but she used the opportunity to launch a diatribe on what I'd done to her standing in the community, what a thoughtless, childish act it had been, whatever the reasons. As a matter of fact, when I reread the letter I could see that the "why" was really an excuse for writing, a means to justify sending a heat-seeking missile to track me down somewhere in America.

I excused myself, went into Tom's study, and found some university stationery on the shelf above his desk. I rolled a sheet through the platin of his ancient typewriter and looked at the keys. I must have stared at the keys for five minutes, twenty-six letters to be arranged in several hundred combinations to explain to Gloria why I was there at that moment trying to explain. I had to put some marks on the piece of paper but I didn't know what they would be. There was only one sure way to begin:

Dear Gloria;

I don't know where to begin. You want to know why I left, and more particularly why I left the way I did, "that melodramatic, childish act," as you put it. Maybe it was melodramatic and childish, but my comic sense of timing has always been off. In this case it was about ten years off. I should have left Brainard and Bancroft Industries ten years ago and taken you with me. I could have done that then. If I'd tried to talk to you about it before I left and asked you to come with me, I would have gotten mired down in details and second thoughts. I never would have done it, and I would have hated myself for my weakness and indecision. Sometimes drama or "melodrama" is the only way. "The courage to strike out on insufficient knowledge," as Frost put it. But I don't need his authority or anyone else's. I left because I had to; and the only reason I can think of that has kept me from doing it all these years was that I didn't want to hurt my father, didn't want to say to him, in effect, "I don't care about Bancroft Industries. I don't care about what you've given your life to. It's not important." I didn't want to say that, mostly because it isn't true. I do care. I'm proud of all that he did and I'm proud of him, not because he built a giant frozen-pie industry but because he didn't lose his humanity doing it, because he was a man, a different sort of man than I wanted or want to be, but a man I respected. I only regret that I lived so long in his shadow, that I never let him see me for what I was, for what I now hope to become, not merely an understudy waiting to take over his part.

My father didn't read poetry, other than Robert Service and a little Longfellow, and he wouldn't have understood what was involved in being or trying to be a poet. But now I know he would have been proud if I'd asserted myself, if I'd really tried. He would have given up on me as an heir, and we could have gotten drunk and gone fishing together. He once told me that he was proud of the success I'd had racing, but that he just couldn't reconcile it with the risk. He didn't really understand it, but it didn't matter. That's the one time I felt I meant something to him as a man. Maybe that's when I should have left.

Everyone assumed I'd keep my nose clean and someday be chairman of the board. Then they'd all say, "Well, what did you expect?" A life's accomplishment of being careful. Well, Bancroft Industries isn't for me. It's a source of income, and I won't knock that (nor will you); but it was important only as an extension of my father, it was kind of his poem, but now he's gone and it's a business and that's all. It'll be taken over by professionals who see it in terms of their careers, another ladder to climb, another raise or stock option. It's inevitable. It's gotten too big, and when anything gets too big it turns into a machine. My father could never bring himself to fire anyone. If the job became too much for a man, he'd find something else for him to do, even if he had to create a job just to keep him on. It was reward for past service, but more than that, he felt too much a part of everyone who worked for him and couldn't turn them out, not very efficient, but very human. But a business can't be that way anymore. It's just a business, a means to producing goods and income. It's not a life's work; it's a job. You don't know what it is to be a small part of something so big you can never see the results of anything you do. It's like spending years racking your brain and ruining your vision carving snowflakes that are instantly blown away in the storm, what it does to kill imagination and one's sense of self to write the same letters day after day, to prepare the same face, to be nice to the right people, to be surrounded by hundreds of other people doing the same kinds of things, to devise little games to keep from going insane, to know that the end of it all is a gold watch and a handshake. They take your name off the door, off the guardrail in the parking lot, and except for your signature on a thousand purchase requisitions stored in black boxes for tax purposes and destroyed after seven years, you cease to exist.

But what's really important is that I'm a poet. I know you'll laugh when you read that. I haven't accomplished it with work yet, with poems, but I will. At the very least I'll be a failed poet. There's always that risk. I should have given myself over to it from the time I first met Claude Larimer and discovered Whitman. I knew then it was what I had to do. But I didn't have the courage.

For thirty-one years I've lived a life that was planned for me, determining everything I've done or considered doing on the basis of what other people would think. Well, I know two things for sure; it's what *I* think that matters, and it's the things I *haven't* done that I regret. I've confined my impulse toward poetry to almost that of a hobby because I've been conditioned to believe that it can't be a respectable life's work. "What if you didn't have money?" That question again and again. The hell with that. The fact is that I do have money. What if I didn't have a right hand? I'd have to learn to write with my left. There seems to be a tacit assumption that if you're born with money you have the responsibility to make more money, as if making money were the reason we were given life. Thomas Jefferson said, "I'll fight wars so my son can plant corn, so his son can write poetry." He didn't let fighting wars become his life's work. What if his guilt-ridden grandson said, "I was born into a peaceful society because my grandfather fought wars. What if I hadn't been born into a peaceful time? Poetry's no work for a man. I owe it to my grandfather to make war." There don't seem to be many people who are willing to accept gracefully what's given them. If I hadn't been born with money I'd be poor, because I know now that it isn't worth spending a lifetime to acquire. Its only value is that it can buy time and travel—both of which I've ungratefully ignored. It's too bad you couldn't have married a sane man. I think I know what that word means now, probably for the first time. When I'm ready I'll come back to you or send for you, and we'll see if you can live with my newfound sanity. You may show this letter to my mother if you like, in fact I wish you would. Maybe it'll help her understand.

Larry

I rolled the last sheet out of the machine and stacked it with the others. I reread the letter and corrected the typos and spelling errors with a ballpoint pen. I folded the sheets, stuffed them into a University of Arizona envelope, and sealed it. I hoped it said what I really wanted to say. There were some stamps on the desk, and I pasted three Eisenhowers on the envelope. They made it look quite official. I sat back and read the spines of the books on the shelf above the desk. I listed the ones I'd read, and discovered I'd read all but one. I always claimed I'd read

War and Peace, but I never actually had. I wondered how many other people who talked about *War and Peace* had never actually read it. Maybe someday everyone alive on earth will have not read *War and Peace*. They'll continue to buy the book and to display it on their shelves and to talk about it, but no one will have read it. Over a long period of time the story is bound to change. Pierre will become a Frenchman, and Natasha an imperious countess. In fifty years everyone will assume it's an exhaustive study of American foreign policy.

17

At Kalab's, Mary Lou laughed too hard at Tom's impressions of me crawling up the stairs after Polly Boland. He did his impressions of John Wayne, Jonathan Winters, Woody Allen, and Johnny Lujack. Nobody could remember ever having heard Johnny Lujack say anything, and I'm sure Mary Lou didn't even know who he was, but she laughed anyway. Her head was resting on the back of the chair, and her beautiful teeth were laughing. Her face was flushed and the cords and muscles in her throat stood out, she was laughing so hard. She held her stomach and doubled up with laughter. It wasn't really that funny, but she was laughing uncontrollably. It was really kind of erotic watching her laugh so hard. Her face flushed from pink to bright red. She was laughing, and the tears were streaming down her cheeks. I was laughing, too, but it wasn't really that funny. The laughter had become contagious. Mostly I was watching Mary Lou. Penny wasn't laughing; I'm sure she'd heard it all before. She sat in the big chair smoking and watching Tom with her demure face. Maybe it was the contrast between Mary Lou and Penny that was so erotic. I imagined being with both of them in a big bed on cool sheets, Mary Lou laughing hysterically and Penny holding me demurely. I was the meat in the sandwich. The vibrations from Mary Lou's laughter were transmitted through my body to Penny, and then Penny began to make vibrations of her own that were transmitted to Mary Lou. I was the innocent space between two radios, between two planets trying to communicate without a common language, a medium, a slave to be used, a buffer between two beautiful women trying to reach each other. It had never occurred to me that it might be Penny and not Tom that Mary Lou had been anxious to see. Their bodies grew warm, then hot. They were actually beginning to singe my skin. Mary Lou still laughing, Penny demurely undulating, Tom's John Wayne voice intruding impersonally like a television set blaring in the corner of a room from which everyone has gone to the beach. Their bodies began to grow in size, and I was a little boy between two Amazons. Their nipples were flushed and glowing, burning me like heating coils. I was lost in their breasts, pressed between them. Now I was a flea in the valley between them, and all was warm and dark.

I heard the first crack. It was like someone cracking a bullwhip behind the house, and then a howl, like a child screaming. The laughing stopped. "What was that?" Tom said, his elbows still out at his sides in midstride of a John Wayne walk. The crack came again, but this time the howl was longer and wavered in its pitch. We all ran through the kitchen to the back of the house. I shoved open the door, and Tom switched on the back-porch light, illuminating the alley. There was a German Shepherd crouched on the grass with its front paws extended, crawling toward a man with a pistol in his hands, crawling toward him as if begging for help. The man raised the pistol, turned his head away from the dog, and fired. The dog jerked as the bullet ripped into its shoulder. The man turned his head and fired again. This time the bullet ripped across the dog's nose, and the howl became muted and guttural. We were all frozen for a moment, not sure of what we were seeing. I felt myself going, hurling off the porch as if I were a linebacker again. I slammed into the man, and he slammed into the side of the house across the alley. The arm with the pistol flew back against the house, and the pistol fired again, shattering a window in the house. I drove my elbow into his face and grabbed the pistol from his hand.

"I had to kill him," the man burbled, holding his mouth. "He was going blind."

The dog had crawled to Tom's porch and was resting its head and one paw on the bottom step. It was breathing heavily, and blood glistened in its fur. Blood ran from its mouth, and the howl came from deep within its body. I ran into the light and held the pistol at arm's length. I sighted the dog's brain and fired. I was momentarily amazed at my shot. The bullet divided the skull with an almost lapidary accuracy. A small split in the center. The dog heaved once deeply, rolled onto its back, and was still. One forepaw waved mechanically, but I knew he was dead. It wasn't like a death on television or in the movies, *bang* and he falls still and dead. The dog had suffered, and it didn't understand. It felt the pain of the bullets and crawled to its master for help, and its master turned his head away and fired one blind shot after another. I turned to the man standing behind me. He was trying to hold back the blood that ran from his lip. "You stupid son of a bitch," I said, pointing the pistol at his belly. I pulled the trigger, and there was a hard metallic click. The gun was empty. The man covered his belly with his arms and looked at the pistol with wide eyes. "You could have killed me. You could have killed me," he said.

"What the fuck do you think you're doing," I said. My mouth was dry.

"The dog was going blind. A man's got to shoot his dog when it goes blind. I wanted to do it before my wife got home."

"A man's not a man if he doesn't. Is that what you think?"

"Well, yeah, it's what a man's got to do."

"Did you ever think of taking him to a vet and having him do the job the right way?"

"Yeah, but he'd charge me ten bucks."

"You stupid, cheap son of a bitch," I said, and threw the pistol as far as I could into the darkness. The man began to cry. "Oh, shut up," I said.

Tom had taken the girls back into the house. "Grab his collar," I said. I took the dog's hind legs, and we carried it across the dark lawn to a hole he'd dug behind the house. He had a lantern in the loose sand by the hole, and he turned it on. We lowered the dog into the hole till it touched bottom. The forepaw waved once more as if saying good-bye, and the man began to fill in the hole. I watched the first shovel of sand thump on the dog's belly and turned and walked back to Tom's house. No one was laughing when I walked back into the house. Penny was smoking furiously; Mary Lou sniffling into a handkerchief, and Tom sat in the corner with a blank stare. Mary Lou looked up and said, "What happened?"

"It was the worst thing I've ever seen. That stupid son of a bitch had seen too many movies. He thought he had to shoot the dog, but he wouldn't look at it to see that his shots were any good. He just shot it to pieces, nicked off one piece after another."

There was a long silence and then Tom said, "You almost killed that dude."

"I know. I felt like it."

"I mean if there'd been one more bullet in that gun, you'd have drilled it right into his solar plexus."

"I know. It's scary. I never thought I could shoot anybody." I wondered how often it happened that way, I mean just like that, to someone who never had any intention of killing a man and then through circumstances found himself with a smoking pistol in his hand. "The way I feel right now, I almost wish there had been another bullet," I said. "Two, in fact."

Mary Lou began crying. Penny said, "I don't blame you. That bastard mistreated that dog ever since he got it." She lit another cigarette, and I went over and put my arm around Mary Lou. Tom walked into the kitchen to make drinks. Mary Lou buried her head in my shoulder and wept. I could taste blood in my throat. I thought of the accident and Gloria, of seeing her through the morphine, of drowning in blood, of the warm, thick, salty fluid clogging my throat and filling my stomach, of the dog trying to howl through the blood in its throat.

Tom brought the drinks. I didn't feel like having a drink, but I drank it and asked for another. There wasn't much to say. Tom put on a Buck Owens record and said, "Larry, listen to these words and try and understand my life."

"I can't," I said. "I'm going home. I'm sorry, I can't listen to anything right now." I thanked Penny for dinner and thanked Tom for everything in Tucson. I told him we'd probably leave in the morning.

"Where you going?" Tom asked.

"I don't know," I said. "Maybe Las Vegas. I've never been to Las Vegas, never seen the Grand Canyon either. Maybe we'll go to the Grand Canyon." There was a long silence. "I'll write to you. I'm sorry it had to end with horseshit." I pointed toward the back of the house.

When we got back to the motel I threw up and felt better. I am capable of killing a man, I thought while vomiting. I dreamt of the dog, of its howling and begging for help, of the blood in my throat and another bullet ripping into me, of the ducks I'd killed when I used to hunt, the ones I found wounded on the water and had to beat their heads against the gunwales of the boat or ring their necks. I dreamed of the man holding his belly and the gun exploding in my hand, the bullet opening his stomach like a stone dropped in a still pool as he fell backward. When I was in Wyoming I'd watched them film *Shane*, the scene where Jack Palance gunned down the squatter named Tory in front of the saloon, saw ten men pull a wire attached to Tory's belt, Tory flying backward into a mud puddle as the shot rang out. They repeated the scene six times to get it right. The man in the alley flew backward holding his belly, and I was laughing. "That's very good," I said. "That's very good." He lay on the gravel screaming and crying. "Okay, you can cut it now," I shouted, but he didn't stop. "You can cut it now." I was petting a cow in the pasture at Aunt Hilda's farm, and I was small. The field was deep, deep green and dotted with yellow cowslips, and I ripped up handfuls of lush grass and fed them to Ann, the cow's name was Ann, and she rolled her jaw as she chewed and rubbed her head up and down my ribs. I was leading her with a rope, a poleaxe came down on her skull, and I was eating steak from a sizzling platter. I dreamed of Anne Boleyn, leading Anne Boleyn to the scaffold, and Lady Jane Grey. I loved Lady

~~~ *115*

Jane Grey and wanted to save her from the headsman. Later I learned that she was a fanatical little bitch and refused to save herself, but when I was twelve I loved her. Her husband of three days was executed just before she was. I wondered if they'd had time to make love and whether if she'd been spared, she would have loved me. The lights went dim, and I felt the straps around my chest, around my wrists and ankles, and the first shock, as I heard the buzz saw rip into the pine.

The room was half light, the sun still behind the mountains, and I thought about Tom and whether I should leave Tucson this way. But I'd decided to go. It would be easier, and when I stayed too long anywhere I thought about home. I was sticky with perspiration, and I took a shower.

PART 3

18

After breakfast we headed north on 10. It was a clear day, and I wondered what would have happened that day if we'd decided to stay. And had I really fucked Polly Boland? I'd never know; but if I had, I was sorry to have missed it.

We got to Phoenix about noon, and the highway exit signs began to flash familiar names; Tempe, Mesa, Chandler. I'd roped claves at Chandler and gone to movies and gang fights in Mesa. We turned off at the Scottsdale exit. I decided to show Mary Lou where I spent one awful year of my adolescence. Scottsdale had changed. When I had lived there it was a separate little town, and now it was part of Phoenix. Phoenix had become a mini-Los Angeles, swallowing up the surrounding towns in urban sprawl. It even had the smog. The sky was no longer clear and blue, but an off-yellow, and the mountains were indistinct as they faded in the brown soup of the sky. People used to come here to get away from it all. Now they've brought it all with them.

Driving past the school was like looking at a prison where one had been formerly incarcerated, feeling at the same time the nausea of unpleasant associations and the exhilaration of no longer being an inmate. It must be similar to the smug assurance of a Marine drill instructor: "I've been through hell, and now I'm going to put you through it." I saw several students wearing jeans and cowboy boots walking toward the dining hall and was glad I was not one of them. The hairdos were different, no D.A.s, and a few new buildings, but that was all. I told Mary Lou about all the movie stars' children and "poor little rich kids," and she said she guessed that having money wasn't all it was cracked up to be. Across the road from the school was the western edge of the Salt River Indian Reservation. I told Mary Lou how I used to ride across the reservation, sometimes riding two or three days, about the shacks and mud huts the Indians lived in, their herds of sheep and decrepit horses, how I slept in the mesquite by the banks of Cave Creek and trotted the horses all the way to make them last longer, about the sores and aches. I told her about the wafer-thin hamburgers that the inmates were probably getting for lunch, and we decided to go to Trader Vic's. I think it was Frank O'Connor who said, "I like to take out my comforts and examine them in the light of other's misfortunes." I like to gloat.

Trader Vic's was in a very chichi part of Scottsdale, just crackling with ermine, papier-mâché, and perfume shops, overwhelmed with its own cuteness. The entire area was built to resemble a Walt Disney western-movie set filled with Saks Fifth Avenue, Bonwit Teller, and Games Imported, everything to amuse the wealthy alcoholic. Every adult I'd met in Scottsdale was an alcoholic or soon to become one. It crossed my mind that I might end up that way. I didn't have a profession. If somebody asked what I did, what could I say? "I'm an escapee from a pie factory," "a family deserter," or "I travel." That's it, "I travel." Everybody has to have a vocational justification, and traveling is better than saying "I drink a lot." Then I remembered Polly Boland and my new title: POET. "I'm a Poet." That's what I told Earl and Honey. We met Earl and Honey at Trader Vic's. The restaurant was crowded, and they didn't have any tables for two, but they did have a table for four. Earl and Honey wanted a table, and Earl introduced himself and suggested we take a table together. Why not?

Earl was a retired sales executive for a novelty company, and he and Honey were "just out West to see the sights and to look over Sun City. We're thinking of buying a little place there for our golden years." Earl was tall and bald and cadaverous. He talked entirely with his lower jaw and slurred his words like Abigail VanBuren. He also chewed with his mouth open. Honey looked like a Gila monster with glasses, a kind of grandmotherly Gila monster.

"We're from Chicago," Earl slurred as we sat down.

"Congratulations," I said.

"Hear that, honey," Earl said chuckling. "He said congratulations."

"I heard, Earl," she said, without moving her mouth.

"What line you in?" Earl asked.

"Poetry."

"Oh. You hear that, honey, he's in poetry."

"My sister writes poetry," Honey said. "Some of it's real nice. She had a poem in *Good Housekeeping* back in the fifties or maybe it was the forties." The rhinestones in her glasses were dazzling me.

"There ain't much money in poetry, is there?" Earl asked.

"I pull down six hundred a week, plus expenses. That's during the off season, of course."

"I never would have imagined," Earl said.

"Neither would he," said Honey. "Young man, I don't think I caught your wife's name."

"Larry," I said.

"My, that's unusual."

"No, Larry's my name. I meant, please call me Larry."

"Oh my, I thought. . . ."

"I know," I said. "I didn't tell you my wife's name because she's not my wife, but her name's Mary Lou."

"Oh lord, you young people today, free as birds, just fussin' around. Earl and I used to fuss around a lot before he had all that trouble with his prostate. Just took the starch out of him. Tell 'em about your prostate, Earl."

"Not now, Honey."

"Oh, Earl's so sensitive about his prostate," Honey said, patting his thigh.

Mary Lou tried to suppress a giggle.

"Earl was with the same company for thirty-five years and never had a bit of trouble with his prostate till he retired."

"That'll do it everytime," I said.

"Say, Larry," Earl broke in. "I don't think I caught your last name."

"Bancroft."

"Bancroft as in pie?"

"Yes, I hear that a lot."

"We knew the pie Bancrofts, didn't we, Earl? Our daughter used to date their son, but he was too short for her."

"Really?" I said.

Mary Lou held her napkin to her face and left the table.

"She has these seizures," I said.

"Oh, my," said Honey. "I hope she's all right. Earl used to sell little plastic-pie keychains to the Bancrofts."

"Best sales gimmick they ever had," said Earl.

I'd had a drawer full of plastic-pie keychains when I was in the sixth grade. On the white plastic back of the pies was printed in red letters, "Bancroft, the humble pie, for those who don't like a lot of crust." It backfired miserably, and the company was stuck with a million and a half keychains. I used to trade them for favors and baseball cards. And now I'd met the source of all my childhood power. I ordered Indonesian Lamb, which turned out to be roast lamb with peanut butter sauce. I decided that thereafter I would always eat my lamb with peanut butter.

Earl and Honey were heading for Las Vegas. "We're going to swing a little," Honey said as we left the restaurant. She winked at me. It wasn't a grandmotherly wink.

"It was real swell to meet you kids," Earl said.

"Same here," I said, "and I hope you break the bank."

"I hope so too," Earl chuckled.

Honey took Mary Lou aside and told her to be sure I took "real good care" of my prostate. Mary Lou assured her I would.

"It means a lot," Honey said. "It really does."

On the way to Flagstaff we talked about what a sweet old couple Honey and Earl were. Live and let live and all that. Mary Lou thought the world would be a better place if more people were as open as Honey and Earl. I said I wouldn't go that far. I was a little tired of the tales of Earl's prostate. That would make a good title for a book, I decided.

There was a thin layer of snow on the ground when we got to Flagstaff. Our room at the Holiday Inn overlooked a trailer park, really a subdivision of big trailers without wheels. "Student housing," the man at the desk told us. There seemed to be an awful lot of students in this world.

Perhaps someday everyone would be a student, and all the buildings would be student housing. The University of the World. There would be no more wars, only campus disturbances; no armies, only the campus police force of forty-eight million men; no presidents or premiers, only department chairmen and deans. An English department, a Russian department, a French department, a Chinese department. Maybe there'd have to be two Chinese departments. There would of course be no American department, and that would put a lot of administrative people out of work, people who couldn't be trained for honest labor. No, they'd have to establish an American department after all, as a kind of catch-all for all those who were dissatisfied with the other departments, an all-university control group, to control all the other departments. A lot of nasty politics could be avoided that way. There would have to be a new system of grading and granting tenure and a re-evaluation of the consequences of flunking out. Armies of cheerleaders modeled after the Red Guard would maintain school spirit with pep rallies, sequenced, of course, to prevent the shattering of the earth's crust by the simultaneous vibration of fourteen billion vocal cords singing "Boola Boola." Oh, there'd be a few administrative problems, I'm sure, but nothing that couldn't be worked out by the student senate with the help of the Phi Delts and the Young Republicans.

I outlined my plan for Mary Lou, but she was tired and less than amused. She wanted to talk about *us* again.

"Larry, what are we doing in Flagstaff, Arizona?"

"What do you mean, what are we doing in Flagstaff, Arizona? We've got to be somewhere. Now it just happens to be here."

"Goddamn it, Larry, you don't have to treat me like a three-year-old. You know what I mean. . . . What are we doing; where are we going; what are we going to do with our lives?"

"For a girl from a cheap bar in Benton Harbor, you sure get uptight about a future you didn't have to begin with. What are you worried about, your pension?"

"Us, Larry, what about us? We can't spend the rest of our lives running away."

"We're not running away, at least I'm not; and it's not the rest of our lives. It hasn't been a month."

"What about me, what about your wife?"

"I don't know what about my wife. I'll deal with her when I have to. You can bail out anytime you want to, you know. Nobody made any promises."

Her eyes were getting teary, her lips quivery and uncertain, and I knew this discussion was about over. Arguing with a weeping woman was, for me, like playing stud poker with the Mafia, using their deck of cards. I put my arms around her and told her I was sorry. I thought about making love to her, but it just wouldn't work. We lay on the bed in each other's arms, thinking our separate thoughts. By calling a tie, I'd won, at least for a while.

After dinner we went back to our room and watched television. Mary Lou was sleepy, and I gave the TV set my unswerving concentration. I don't remember any of the programs, but I was beginning to form a theory about commercials and the cycles of our cultural and religious heritage. All of the products advertised themselves. There were no John Cameron Swayzes to tell us about Timex watches, no Ted Macks to tell us about Geritol. The glowing tube flashed one hundred and twenty-seven electronically divided lines depicting antipollution valves selling gasoline, carburetors that talked to fuel pumps and oil sumps, stomachs that talked to flu bugs, cats who told their masters what to feed them, talking loaves of bread trying to sell themselves, anthropoid tuna fish begging to be eaten, children wishing they were hot dogs. My mind completed the obvious syllogism of a little boy finding his way to his girl friend's belly, not through her vagina but through her digestive tract, disguised as an Oscar Meyer weiner. You can imagine what finally became of him, transformed by love into a useless turd. The ultimate in oral sex.

Finally there was a talking wad of dough that laughed when a finger poked his spongy belly. I instantly felt the urge to divide him with a machete. We were making a complete cycle. The anthropomorphic gods of the ancient Greeks were again emerging as the end products of a consumer economy in which we'd made gods out of things and, like the ancient Greeks, ultimately we desired to become gods or godlike, striving through endless imitation. *I Went to Heaven as a Hot Dog,* by Larry Bancroft. My biography lay before me.

At last, a commerical with people. A man passes a woman on the street and fails to recognize her. She calls to him, and he says, "Lois, is that really you?" "Cross my heart," she says, making a big X on her breast. It turns out the reason he didn't recognize her was that she was wearing a new bra. I ran it by again: "My God, Lois, is that really you? Your tits are so big, I didn't recognize them." Then a commercial for a feminine hygiene deodorant spray. Late night TV. A friend of mine suggested a male genital spray called "Foul Ball."

At two A.M. I discovered there was a railroad track just the other side of the student trailer park, and the mountain rising behind it cupped the sound and fired it at the motel like a giant amplifier. Unlike the distant train in Tucson, this one didn't carry me back to my hobo-dream-world childhood. It kept me awake. I must have finally drifted off to sleep, because about dawn I woke up to sloshing sounds coming from the bathroom. I looked over, saw Mary Lou still sleeping, and stumbled to the bathroom door. It was the maid, an Indian woman of about fifty, just finishing mopping the floor. The bowl and basin were sparkling, and there was even one of those paper bands around the toilet seat that said, *For your personal protection.* She picked up her bucket and said matter-of-factly that she'd come back and make up the beds when we were out of them.

"That's very considerate," I said. She didn't even seem to notice I was naked. I didn't notice it either until after I'd closed the door behind her. At first I felt a little silly; but then, thinking about it, I was a little hurt that she hadn't reacted with a scream and run from the room covering her eyes. Did I appear completely harmless? I went and stood before the mirror, but I decided I wasn't the one to judge. I'd grown so used to me I was boring. I woke up Mary Lou and told her about it, and she laughed and said I had it coming. She thought it was funny, funnier than it really was.

19

I couldn't get used to the idea of the Grand Canyon sprinkled with snow. All the movies I'd seen of it were shot in the summer to the tune of "The Donkey Serenade." "Thank you, Johnny, I'll have a pack of Phillip Morris." The Phillip Morris Canyon. How barren my childhood would have been without radio. We stopped at Desert View Point. It was cold, and we were alone. We tried to guess the distances across the canyon. The spectacular beauty was beginning to depress me.

We walked out on the point to get a really good view, the canyon disappeared. It was snowing, and we might as well have been in Michigan. All we could see was each other. We groped back to the car and drove west along the south rim. We stopped for lunch at the South Rim Lodge, which reminded me of the 1940s idea of a ski lodge, log cabin construction, stained dark brown and smelling of creosote, with large fireplaces and stone floors. Very cozy. I expected Greta Garbo and Melvyn Douglas to breeze out of the dining room. I perused the souvenir store and remembered when souvenirs were my consuming passion. I found a paperback Rimbaud in the pocket of my parka and snuck a few *Illuminations* in with my

Lobster Newburg and glanced out the window as the snow cleared. It seemed incongruous to be eating lobster at the Grand Canyon. The only conversation was Mary Lou saying, "Gee, here we are at the Grand Canyon." I offered to buy a sticker for the car, but she refused to answer.

At first I thought there was a carnival in town and then realized it was simply Las Vegas. It would be a wondrous sight to anyone who couldn't read. When I first walked into the hotel lobby I thought I'd stumbled into a glamorous tool-and-die factory. Lines of middle-aged women at slot machines who would have made good drill-press operators. Maybe they were vacationing drill-press operators, and pulling that lever was the only movement they were trained for. We went to the desk, and I was just signing the register when I felt a hand on my shoulder and heard Earl's unmistakable, mouth-full-of-marbles voice, "Say, young feller, fancy meeting you here." At first I thought he'd been hired as an official greeter for the Chamber of Commerce. His bald pate was covered with an enormous white Stetson that matched his long white sideburns.

"Honey and I were just talking about you two and looked over and there you were."

"Why don't you kids have dinner with us to celebrate our reunion. You just go ahead and get settled in your room, and we'll meet you in the dining room over there." I looked in the direction he indicated and saw Honey winking and waving from an overstuffed imitation red velvet sofa.

"Our reunion, by all means," I said.

For a moment I thought I might feel conspicuous in my Levi's and hunting boots, but when we got to the dining room I realized that everyone was in costume anyway. I decided to be an exiled Russian count presently residing in Oregon. Honey greeted Mary Lou and me each with a big wet kiss. Mary Lou's was on the cheek, but mine was on the lips and held a little too long to be considered grandmotherly. There was a lot of talk about what a coincidence it was that we both chose the same hotel, and we compared notes on the Grand Canyon. As it turned out, Honey and Earl had spent the night at the same lodge where I had eaten the Lobster Newburg, and Honey went into ecstasies over that.

After dinner there was a floor show, and Honey patted my thigh with delight every time Bobby Darin sang "Yeah, Yeah, Yeah." We had a lot of drinks, wine with dinner, and brandy in big snifters. Earl had a big cigar. "Cuban," he chuckled as he winked through the flame of his butane lighter.

"Say," Honey said, pressing her hand on mine, "Earl and I were wondering if you two would like to play a little switcharoo?"

"Pardon me?" I said, not sure what I'd heard.

"You know," Honey continued, "a little hanky-panky. I could show you a thing or two, Larry, and it'd be so good for Earl's prostate."

Mary Lou and I looked at each other, too stunned to laugh. Mary Lou looked at the ceiling and squinted as if she were intently studying the ventilation system. Honey and Earl sat poised on the edge of their chairs, waiting for a reaction with that "What do ya say?" look.

"Well," I said. That was all I could say.

"Well, just think of the fun it would be," Honey said. "Explore a little new territory." She punched me in the ribs.

Discover the Old World, I thought.

"You could just sneak up to our room with me," she went on, "and Mary Lou there could just drift off with Earl." I tried to imagine Mary Lou *drifting off with Earl* and couldn't. I wondered if he'd remove his Stetson in bed. I looked at Mary Lou, and she was still studying the ceiling.

"Well, the fact is," I said, pausing to clear my throat, "I've got this infectious gonorrhea I haven't been able to shake, and for all we know, Mary Lou's got it, too." I looked at Mary Lou, and she'd finished investigating the ventilation system and was trying to suppress a giggle in her napkin.

"Oh, dear, that's a rotten shame," Honey said, her rhinestone rims sparkling with concern. She patted my hand. "Earl and I went through that once. It was a bad time, but I think it really brought us closer together. Adversity has a way of doing that, you know."

Mary Lou's laughter broke out of her napkin and rose to an almost hysterical intensity. Her face turned red, and she was having trouble breathing.

"Oh, dear, now you've upset her," Honey said. "It's all right dear, a little penicillin will take care of everything."

I got up from the table and helped Mary Lou to her feet. "Another of her seizures, I'm afraid," I said. "Thanks for the dinner, Earl. It was swell seeing you." I put my arm around Mary Lou as if I were helping her walk. Earl removed his Stetson and held it to his chest, and Honey squinted with concern. Mary Lou and I couldn't stop laughing even when we got back to our room.

"Did you feel old age creeping up on you?" she asked, running spider fingers over my body. "I can show you a thing or two, young feller," she said, winking and sliding her hand into my trousers.

The slot machines were whirling and clicking when we went down for breakfast, and those that stood idle looked like chromium tombs. When the elevator door opened on the lobby I was mooned by a woman in white slacks, looking up a payoff chute as if she were checking the machine for hemorrhoids. It was an enormous expanse of white and ruined my whole day. In the restaurant we were encouraged to play Bingo with breakfast, and I knew I couldn't stay. It seemed to me I'd seen all these people before in Miami Beach, and they still looked jaded and bored. "Goddamn it, Irving, we saved a year for this vacation, and you're going to enjoy it whether you like it or not."

We got an early start down 15 through the desert into California. We realized we were both almost desperate to reach the ocean, as if after weeks of idle wandering we had entered a magnetic field, and the attraction grew steadily stronger. "I wonder if this is how it begins with lemmings," I said, and then had to explain to Mary Lou about lemmings and their suicidal rush to the sea.

We took the freeway all the way to Santa Monica Beach, "Sanamonica" as the natives call it, and drove south along the ocean. Melville must have been right about the natural attraction of water. It seemed everyone was trying to live on the water, piled together and on top of each other as if a child had dumped an enormous container of blocks in the sand and strung them endlessly down the beach.

Mary Lou kept saying, "That's really the Pacific Ocean?" She said it again and again. She'd never seen an ocean before but thought it looked just like Lake Michigan.

"It is just like Lake Michigan," I said, "except it's five thousand miles across, and there's no Milwaukee on the other side." I thought of Lake Michigan and the early

March storms that must be piling up miniature mountain ranges of ice along the eastern shore. I used to walk on the ice and dodge the spray from volcanoes as the wind drove water under the ice, shooting it up through cracks and fissures to form conical hills of frozen spray.

The sun was getting low toward the south, not yet red, but the water had taken on its soft late-afternoon glare. We checked into a motel in Hermosa Beach and drove south to Palos Verdes. The road climbed high on the hills, and we could see Santa Catalina Island in the haze. Mary Lou asked how far out it was to the island, and I sang a few bars of "Twenty-six miles across the sea, Santa Catalina is a-waitin' for me, Santa Catalina, the island of romance, romance, romance, romance." We drove to San Pedro and had dinner at a Polynesian restaurant on the water. All the waiters wore flowered shirts and talked like sailors. Ships passed, shadows moving across the lights from the other side of the harbor. Mary Lou wanted to see Hollywood, and I promised to take her to Schwab's drugstore where she might be discovered as Lana Turner had been.

It was windy that night, and the next morning the Santa Ana Mountains seemed much closer than they had the previous afternoon. It was mildly startling. We drove to Point Vicente and stopped at Marine Land of the Pacific. We watched performing dolphins and pilot whales, and Mary Lou fell in love with a sea lion. If she couldn't have an otter, she'd take a sea lion, she decided. In the afternoon we toured Universal City Studios on an open bus with a girl guide whom I suspected of having been an ex-Mouseketeer. She rattled off an animated spiel as if it had been recorded and she was only moving her lips. It was a big letdown to see the shell of the house where Tony Perkins had played his psychotic dead mother in *Psycho*, the home of Marcus Welby, M.D., behind imitation shrubs and trees that could be re-ordered at will, the Western town where all the doorways were scaled to seven-eighths size to make actors look larger and more epic. Did they have to destroy all my illusions? Finally there was a flash flood, summoned up with recorded thunder and synthetic lightning, which rushed down a hillside trough and drained systematically into well-placed sewers, gone as suddenly as it had begun, with only a few glistening wet rocks to show it had ever been. It left me dissatisfied and hungry for a real downpour, one that would really threaten me. We drove up Laurel Canyon, and I showed Mary Lou where Houdini had lived and told her the story of the mysterious light that always burned in the abandoned house. I made up the story, but it was so good that I felt relieved when we got out of the dark, cool canyon.

We had a dinner of brown rice and carrot juice at a health food restaurant near the Farmer's Market. It didn't make me feel particularly healthy, just left me hungry; and we stopped for a pizza an hour later. We saw *Little Big Man*, found Shirley Temple's little handprints at Grauman's Chinese Theatre, and went to Schwab's drugstore for a soda, but nothing happened. No one offered Mary Lou a screen test, but the soda was good and we were both tired. We drove back to Hermosa Beach and fell asleep watching television.

20

It was on the riverboat ride at Disneyland that Mary Lou started talking about *us* again, about our future or lack of it. I didn't want it to come to a showdown. I loved Mary Lou. I think I did. I was irritated by her insistence and started talking like Bugs Bunny, puffing up my cheeks to make a moustache, but it didn't work. She didn't even smile.

"Larry, you can't just make a game out of it. It won't just all go away."

"Why not, Doc, tch, tch, tch, tch, tch, it tastes pretty good to me."

"Goddamn it, Larry, can't you ever be serious about anything?"

"Yes, I can. I'm serious about wanting to do a good Bugs Bunny. It is good, isn't it?"

"Yes. No. I don't know. I suppose it's good if it helps you forget reality." Her cheeks were getting puffy, and she was close to tears. "But I can't forget about it. You've got a wife and two children back in Michigan, and you're going to have to face that sooner or later."

"I'll take it later, thank you."

"It'll always be later." She stumbled a moment looking

for words. "Larry, I'm tired of being your mistress. It's got to be all or nothing."

"Well, I'd say that's pretty goddamn provincial. It was okay to be a whore in Benton Harbor, but all of a sudden the term 'mistress' is more than you can bear." I realized I was shouting.

"I was not a whore," she cried.

Parents and children with sticky little hands were staring at us. One fat man in argyle socks and madras Bermuda shorts looked out from under his sunglasses and souvenir baseball cap and said, "Why don't you conduct your private business in private. There're decent people here."

"Why don't you and your decent people get fucked," I shouted.

The riverboat had docked, and I grabbed Mary Lou's hand and pulled her down the gangway. We didn't speak until we got to the car. I pulled onto the Santa Ana Freeway and headed north. The sound of the tires whirring, and the air rushing by the windows was maddening. When Mary Lou spoke, it startled me. "I hope you're proud of that little scene," she said.

"You know what that sounds like. That sounds just like Gloria. I don't have to make a decision. The decision's made for me. I've a shrew here and a shrew at home."

"Well, I'm not Gloria, goddamnit, Larry."

"No, you're not. Gloria doesn't swear."

"Now who's being righteous and provincial?"

"Oh, shut up."

When we got to the motel Mary Lou grabbed my arm as I started to get out of the car. "Larry, I love you, but I've made up my mind. If you don't do something about Gloria, tell her you're leaving her, go home, and get this all straightened out, I'm leaving you."

"No, you're not leaving, goddamnit, because I am." I slammed the car door and went to the room and began packing my things. Mary Lou followed me. She stood by the door sniffling.

"Larry, don't go," she said as I walked out the door. I put my bag in the car and reached under the seat and took ten one-hundred-dollar bills from the cache. I went back to the room and threw the money on the bed.

"There," I said, "that'll hold you. I'm sure you won't have any trouble latching on to someone else." I could hear her crying as I walked away. I knew I'd been unnecessarily cruel, but I was determined to make the scene work. I drove down the Coast Highway to Harbor City and went to a bar. It had dark wood paneling and a dirty linoleum floor. The late-afternoon sun came through two small pillbox windows and sparkled off the bottles behind the bar. The bartender wore a dirty white apron and chewed gum with his mouth open.

"Where you from?" the mouth asked.

"Michigan," I said, absently. All I could see was the gum rolling in the rictus of his face.

"I didn't think I'd seen ya around," he said.

I had a double gin-and-tonic and punched a couple of James Taylor songs on the jukebox. The second song turned out to be Tammy Wynette singing "D-I-V-O-R-C-E." I must have punched the wrong button, or maybe I hadn't. I laughed to myself and ordered another double. I drove back to Palos Verdes and watched the sun getting low over Catalina. It had been two hours. I figured that was long enough. Mary Lou would have had time to simmer down, and she'd be so happy to have me back she'd forget about Gloria for a while. I hadn't forgotten about Gloria, but I just didn't know what to do about Gloria. As I drove into Hermosa Beach I wondered if

Mary Lou would give the the money back. "Oh, hell, let her keep it," I thought. "With what I put her through she earned it." I parked in front of the motel and knocked on the door of our room, but there was no answer. I pounded on the door and hollered for her to let me in, but there still wasn't any answer. I heard the lock snap just as I was about to go to the office for the key. The door opened a crack, still secured by the night chain and an eye looked out at me from the dark room. "Mary Lou," I said, and then I could see it wasn't Mary Lou's eye. It was a man's eye, bloodshot and wide.

"What do you want?" he whispered.

"Mary Lou," I said. It was all I could think of.

"This ain't Mary Lou in here," the man said, tipping his head toward the darkness behind him. "Now get lost."

He slammed the door, and I ran to the office. "Room 112, a tall blonde girl. Where is she?"

"I don't know," the clerk said. "She checked out a couple of hours ago."

"Where did she go?" I demanded.

"I told you I don't know. I called her a cab, and she paid your bill and walked out. She's your wife, you ought to know where she went."

I considered punching him in the snotlocker, but I just didn't have the energy. I couldn't believe she'd really gone. Where would she go? She could be anywhere in Los Angeles. She was probably on her way back to Benton Harbor. "Home is where, when you have to go there, they have to take you in," I thought. I went to a bar down the street and had three more doubles. I didn't know where to begin. She didn't know anybody in Los Angeles. Neither did I. I walked to the beach and looked at the glow in the sky where the sun had been. I sat in the sand and dug trenches with my heels. I noticed my bootlaces were tied in double knots. I'd always tied my laces in double knots, ever since I could remember. It was just the way I was taught to tie them. Someone told me once that I tied double knots because I was insecure. Maybe they were right. I considered calling Gloria but decided not to. I didn't even know if she was still there. I considered the double-knot habit. Maybe if I stopped tying my shoelaces in double knots I wouldn't be insecure anymore. Maybe I'd change my handwriting and thereby change my personality. I thought of all my self-improvement binges. My Charles Atlas dynamic tension course, my Joe Wieder barbells. I actually put on forty pounds with the barbells, but after I stopped working out and playing football it all turned to fat, and I had to undertake a self-improvement diet to get my clothes to fit again. I took a speed-reading course, but got bored with all the dull articles I had to read with a stopwatch in one hand and went back to crawling through Lorca and Nabokov. I signed up for a Famous Writer's course. I had visions of myself there in the picture with Rod Serling and Faith Baldwin and all those other famous writers I couldn't really bring myself to read, my desk bristling with pencils, reams of corrasable bond, my agent calling to tell me the "Today Show" wants me and will reschedule Pauline Fredricks and the United Nations at my convenience, lunch at 21 with my editor, fan letters from Jean Simmons, it was Jean Simmons at the time. But the nameless dodo who sent back my first story only commented on my spelling and punctuation. My second and final story was about a hack writer who couldn't write and finally, in desperation, took a job with the Famous Writer's School. I never heard back from them, and I never paid. I tried a Berlitz home French course, I tried to improve my vocabulary, I tried to learn to spell but discovered that I had a mild dyslexia and couldn't tell left from right. The American Genius syndrome.

I was finally on the right track, I decided. I'd read somewhere that pleasure converts to energy and remembered that Blake said, "Energy is genius." Therefore pleasure must convert to genius. Again I'd confirmed that the pleasantest path is usually the right one. Hail John Stuart Mill, hail hedonistic utilitarianism, hail pleasure and genius. I was cold and the sky was black, I went back to the bar, had five more doubles, crawled in the Porsche, and went to sleep.

21

I had a severe headache in the morning. I'd forgotten that gin in quantity gives me a headache. It wasn't severe enough to make me swear off gin. With all its adverse side effects it's still my favorite booze. The only thing that could make me swear off was nausea. I'd sworn off dozens of times while tossing my cookies. It was painful and degrading and filled my mouth with a foul substance I'd never dream of putting there voluntarily. It was also hard to catch my breath. "Please, God, make me well and I'll never drink again, till next time." But this morning it was just a headache. I really didn't feel it till I tried to get out of the car. Then my brain began to quiver and scrape against the boney, abrasive inner walls of my skull. I tiptoed to the restaurant across the street and bought an Alka-Seltzer. I eased back to the beach and sat in the sand. It was already late morning and quite warm. Several people were sunbathing, and the ocean was almost glassy. If there'd been any surf I suppose the surfers would have been surfing. That's the picture I always had when I dreamed of California. I expected to see lots of nubile Gidgets playing volleyball on the beach while their hot dogs (a euphemism I'm still not sure I understand) were out riding the wild surf. I'd seen lots of surfboard shops in Los Angeles but no surfers and no surf.

As the sun began to penetrate my clothes, my headache began to dissolve, and I started thinking about Mary Lou. I was really quite comfortable in the warm sand. I figured this was as good a place as any to look for her. If she decided to come back, this was where she was most likely to come. Besides, the scenery was improving. I noticed that not twenty feet away someone had spread a towel on the sand and was preparing to lie on it. Moreover, that someone was wearing a two-piece international-orange bikini. I knew it was international orange because it was the color of the Golden Gate Bridge, and I'd read in a magazine that the Golden Gate Bridge was constantly being painted with international-orange paint to keep it golden. I'd go to San Francisco, I decided, but not today. I wasn't going anywhere today. The person in the orange bikini had long straight black hair, like the girls on Tahitian travel posters, and a very dark suntan. She was coated with oil and glistened in the sun. I imagined trying to hold onto her oily body. She kept popping out of my arms and zipping across an endless plain of white satin sheets. Teasing me like a mirage. She lay down on her back and twisted her hair in a ball beside her head. In her new posture, her stomach sunk below the level of her rib cage emphasizing the rise and curve of her *mons veneris*. There were two little tunnel openings by the points of her hip bones where the flesh dipped before the rise to the center of her abdomen. Her eyes were closed and she was going into her sun trance. I moved closer. She reminded me of an artist's conception of the ancient Aztec's ritual sacrifice of a virgin to the corn god I'd seen in the *National Geographic*. I think it was the corn god. Maybe it was the Incas. She had the most perfect navel I'd ever seen, like a fingerhole in dough. I edged closer, slipping over the sand silently like a sidewinder. There were tiny freckles sprinkled about her collarbone, and I could see the edge of white skin where her breasts dove into their little orange tents. Her aquiline nose glistened, and she wiggled it as if it itched. She lifted her head, making a visor with her hand, and looked at me. She blinked her eyes as if she were just waking up. They were violet.

"Hey, you're casting a shadow, buster," she said in a soft deep voice.

"Oh, I am?" I said, looking around. On that vast, almost empty stretch of beach, I'd moved so close to this sun-worshiper that I'd come between her and the sun.

"I'm sorry, I hadn't noticed," I said.

"Well, move it." This time the voice was definitely masculine. I looked again closely and determined that the *mons veneris* was distinctly lumpy. I was dazed.

"Are you going to move out of my sun or am I going to have to move you?"

"I'm sorry, sir, uh, madam." I got up and walked away, turning several times to look back. The person in the orange bikini flashed an uncomplimentary sign with his middle finger. Maybe I will go to San Francisco today, I thought. I returned the sign and ran for my car, badly shaken. I'd almost fallen in love with him. I wanted to tell someone about it. I considered calling Gloria but decided I'd have to lay too much groundwork, do too much explaining before I told her of my transsexual adventure at Hermosa Beach. I thought about telling the waitress at the restaurant across the street but ordered a cheeseburger instead. It occurred to me that I hadn't eaten since lunch the day before at Disneyland.

I drove north on Highway 1 and picked up 101 at El Rio. The fabled highways of America. I tried to remember the words to "Black Leather Jacket and Motorcycle Boots" but, apart from the title, all I could summon up was, "that fool was the terror of Highway 101." That was the important part. When I was in high school wearing my black leather jacket, I'd made every road "Highway 101." I always traveled with theme music and imagined I was Marlon Brando. Now the best I could do was Larry Bancroft on my way from one city where I knew no one to another city where I was unknown. And somewhere back there or out there, somewhere, was Mary Lou. Maybe she was sorry now she hadn't waited for me, maybe she had been convinced I wasn't coming back, maybe I'd been too cruel and destroyed whatever feeling she had for me.

It was dusk when 101 met the shore again at Grover City, and I stopped for the night. I sat and wept in my motel room for half an hour after I checked in, then decided I was hungry. I've always had a good dramatic sense, but I also live by my stomach. The tears were genuine; I was genuinely sorry for myself but also genuinely hungry. I remember once battling eight-foot waves in a small boat on Lake Michigan, and the only thought that plagued me wasn't the possibility of drowning but the possibility of being wrecked or driven ashore somewhere where all I could get to eat was a deviled-ham sandwich. I hate deviled ham.

In the morning I switched on the television and discovered it was Sunday. Fifty gap-toothed girls in 1955 junior prom formals were singing, "Fifty Nifty United States," on an evangelist program that advertised tours of Rhodesia and The Holy Land and anticommunist chicken houses for lepers in South Korea. It was hard for me to think of America as "nifty"; maybe these people thought God was nifty. I tried to imagine the pudgy preacher calling his people together to offer the Lord a nifty prayer. I sat in front of the glowing tube, half hypnotized. A disinterested third party looking in on the scene might have thought he was witnessing my salvation. But I frequently sat hypnotized in front of the "Ted Mack Original Amateur Hour" or any afternoon soap opera. The truth is I'm addicted to all kinds of awfulness. I'd rather sit and shiver with embarrassment for the poor saps doing chicken imitations, flapping their elbows and playing "Lady of Spain" on the accordion, than see Olivier's *Hamlet* or Elke Sommer in *Soft Skin on Black Silk*.

I cut off on old Highway 1 and followed it up the coast, relieved that I'd escaped a career in television, then reflected that I didn't have a career in anything. I was an unemployed ex-sales services supervisor. I might as well have been an unemployed buggy whip. Maybe someday I'd settle down, go back to school and be a doctor, or learn to do something useful with my hands. When the toilet backs up you need a plumber. I couldn't recall ever having been needed. I'd been an embarrassment to my parents, an amusement to my friends, and a trial to my wife. I wouldn't even learn to play golf to please her. But now I was driving on Highway 1, and nobody but I knew that. Fuck 'em, fuck 'em all, I decided.

It was foggy along the shore. The sun faded through and seemed to hang in the clouds like a liberated baloon. "Oh, decapitated sun." I had visions conjured up by *The Rhyme of the Ancient Mariner*. Now I was driving through Big Sur, where years ago I'd dreamed of living a bohemian life with Kim Novak. I didn't know what bohemian meant, but I'd thought about taking up pottery. It almost rhymed with poetry. When I was in college I wanted to be a beatnik, but I didn't know what that meant either. The best I could do was to wear my sweatshirts inside out, listen to a lot of jazz, and read Descartes. I really had to read Descartes for a course in systematic philosophies, but I carried the book conspicuously and called everybody "man." I even bought some bongo drums but I only developed one rhythm.

I spent the night near Monterey and took the famous seventeen-mile drive. I walked around Carmel and looked in the windows of exclusive little shops. "Gloria would love this," I thought. It was cool and foggy and chichi and lonely. The next morning I loafed along the beach and listened to the seals on the offshore rocks. I briefly considered a career in zoology and wondered how one went about writing articles for the *National Geographic*. I got back on the highway in late morning and drifted past the firing ranges at Ford Ord. Except for all the targets, it reminded me of the dunes by Lake Michigan where I played as a child. I dug pits in the sand and mounted a toy machine gun made out of a section of cedar fencepost. It was supposed to be a Thompson water-cooled model. The Japs never came, but almost every day Navy Corsairs and Grumman Hellcats flew along the beach so low I could see the pilots' faces or thought I could. "Our boys," I'd say to myself, mark them down in my log book, and resume my visual scan for Zeros. V.J. Day came on my sister's birthday. I wasn't sure what it meant, but my father climbed to the roof of the woodshed and rang the dinner bell till my mother begged him to stop. The next day I resumed my surveillance over the lake, if not for the Japs, then for somebody.

I stopped for lunch at a drive-in restaurant in Castroville, which the sign said was the "Artichoke Capital of the World." *My heart is an interminable artichoke,* I thought and ordered an artichoke burger, french-fried artichokes, and artichokes sautéed in mayonnaise, an artichoke orgy.

I drove away feeling bilious. The seemingly endless fields of artichokes reminded me of the muck farms in Michigan.

I passed Candlestick Park and saw the stacked box houses lining the hillsides I'd come to recognize from photographs of San Francisco. The Porsche was filthy, and so was I. I checked in at the Fairmont, mostly because I liked the name, and the ornate facade of the building gave me a sense of security. I took a shower and put on a clean pair of Levi's. My room was on the third floor and looked out over the main entrance and the parking lot. I looked out the window long enough to convince myself I was really in San Francisco and then went down to the bar.

22

When I entered the bar, the first thing I noticed in the dim light was a woman wearing a coonskin cap with a raccoon face on the front of it. She motioned me to come to her. The raccoon's nose overhung the line of her nose and reminded me of an ancient Greek helmet. I walked to the bar where she was sitting and stared into the sad and beady glass eyes of the former raccoon.

"Young man," she said, "would you please take this to the front desk and ask the clerk if there are any messages for 507."

"Sure," I said, without thinking. I was still looking at the coon's glass eyes. Her voice had an adamantine quality I'd come to associate with a movie about a despotic lady Texas rancher. I turned and walked to the desk with a blind obeisance. "No messages," I told her when I returned.

"Sit down and have a drink," she said, pointing to the stool next to her. "Rockwell, fix this young man a whisky sour."

"But I'd rather have a gin-and-tonic," I said.

"Okay, Rockwell, make that a gin-and-tonic." She turned to me and said, "Don't you know gin is bad for you?" Before I could reply, she snapped, "What's your name, boy?"

"Larry," I said, still comatose.

"Larry. I like that. It's got a nice clean sound, not sterile, but crisp."

"I hope so," I said.

She got up from the stool and said, "Come with me."

"But my drink," I said, motioning toward the icy fizzing glass that Rockwell was just setting on the bar.

"Forget it, drinks are for a man's leisure time," she said. "I'll buy you another."

The Innocent followed her out of the bar and through the lobby to the elevators. She entered the elevator and faced the front. She didn't even look at him. "Five," she said with authority. They walked to the end of a long corridor and stood before a door marked 507. She handed him her key and said, "Open it."

It was an elegant suite with a large crystal chandelier and a low mosaic table in the center of the sitting room. "Wait here," she said and disappeared into the bathroom. He heard water running and a lot of sloshing around. He looked at the prints on the walls, mostly fox-hunting scenes and a Currier and Ives of men cutting ice from a lake and loading it on a sleigh. He wondered what her name was. He turned around when he heard the door open, and she was wearing a long silk robe.

"What's your name?" the Innocent asked. Somehow in the present situation it sounded naive.

"Mrs. Randolph Huntington," she said, "but please call me Mona." He really looked at her for the first time. She'd taken off the coonskin cap, he was thankful for that, and her hair was dark with a few streaks of gray. She looked fiftyish, but well-preserved. She took his hand and led him to a corner of the room. "Take off your boots," she said. He had a difficult time taking his boots off while standing. He hopped around on one foot and tugged at the other, and Mona laughed loudly. "You could have sat on the floor," she said.

The Innocent didn't think it was all that funny and began to wonder what he was doing there anyway. "Come here," she said again. He walked to the chair in which she was sitting. She reached up, unbuttoned his shirt, and ran her hands over his chest. He felt like a piece of merchandise, but enjoyed it in some masochistic sense. He'd frequently imagined being bought as a love slave, particularly in that period when Nat King Cole was singing "Hadji Baba." A male Scheherazade. Mona tugged at his belt till it came undone. She unzipped his fly. He didn't know what to do with his eyes and alternated glances at the frieze around the ceiling and the top of her head. She slid his Levi's and undershorts down with one motion, and he stepped out of them. He was glad his undershorts were clean. She cupped her hand under his balls and stood up. She put her hand gently around his member and led him to the darkened bedroom.

She was proficient in bed in a way he'd never known. She seemed to radiate a piquant aroma that made him dizzy. It was as close to being raped as he'd ever come. The ideal mother turned in disgust and stormed from the room of his mind. Afterward they were silent for a long time. She got out of bed and opened the curtains. She came back, lay on her belly, and examined his face. She took his head in her hands and rotated her thumbs around his temples, then gave him a long kiss. She got up, put on her robe, walked into the sitting room and returned with his Levi's and undershorts, held them out to him and said, "Tomorrow afternoon at three o'clock."

"Wait a minute," the Innocent said.

"Tomorrow at three," she interrupted.

He pulled on his shorts and Levi's and picked up his shirt off the chair in the sitting room. He didn't stop to put on his boots because Mona was standing in the bedroom doorway watching him. He passed a waiter in the hall. At first he didn't understand why the waiter was staring at him. Then he realized his shirt was unbuttoned and he was carrying his boots in his hand.

"I'm late," the Innocent said, nodding and smiling. Luckily the elevator was waiting on the fifth floor, and the doors closed on the staring waiter.

I stopped by my room to finish dressing, returned to the bar and asked Rockwell to make me the gin-and-tonic I'd been previously denied. I drank several and tried to sort it all out in my mind. Mrs. Randolph Huntington. All I knew about her was that her friends called her Mona, she smelled good, and knew what she wanted. She had eclipsed my wildest fantasy. I could hear Mary Lou laughing at me, showing her beautiful teeth to the sky. "I'm sorry, Mary Lou," I said to myself. "I couldn't help it. I've been used." I'd have given anything to have Mary Lou there. But she wasn't there, she was somewhere in Los Angeles, or probably back in Michigan. Why had I given her the money? Without the money she couldn't have gone anywhere. I thought of Gloria. I thought of being home by the fire with my dogs and children. I thought of a necktie around my neck and my wingtip shoes. I felt the cold steel collar tighten at my throat. I asked Rockwell for another drink. I considered asking him about Mona, but reasoned that he probably worked for her and would put the muscle on me for the slightest innuendo. Maybe she owned the hotel. Randolph Huntington sounded like a name that could own a hotel. Larry Bancroft sounded like a name that could own a pair of Jockey shorts or a topless drive-in. Lawrence Bancroft was better. I wondered what Mona would have thought of Lawrence: "Lawrence, I like that. It's dirty, not infectious but distinctly soiled." No, Lawrence seemed a more fitting match for Mrs. Randolph Huntington, but I'd already told her Larry. Who did she think she was anyway?

The next afternoon I presented myself at room 507 precisely at three o'clock. After we'd made love till I was as useless as a wart, she lay with her head on my shoulder and twirled her fingers through the hair on my chest. At that moment she seemed like a little girl. I could feel her hair against my cheek and her slack breasts against my ribs. One thigh lay across my limp groin. I was relaxed and felt at ease with her. If I smoked, I would have had a cigarette then. If I'd had some grass it would have been fun to smoke it with her. I bet she'd never turned on. Maybe she had. There probably wasn't much she hadn't tried.

"Where's Mr. Huntington?" I asked, then immediately wished I hadn't.

Mona lifted her head and looked at me. "Larry, you're a nice boy. I hope you don't begin to bore me."

"I think I've got a right to know," I said.

"Know what?"

"Know something about you. It's not as if we're strangers."

"We are strangers. Just because you know my body, doesn't mean you know me. I prefer to keep it that way."

"I mean I think I've at least got a right to know if your husband might bust in at any moment and threaten to kill me."

"Don't worry about that. My husband's not the type

to bust in. Sometimes I wish he were." She lay her head back on my shoulder and stroked my chest. "We're safe," she whispered. "We're safe."

The three o'clock visits became a daily routine. Sometimes we didn't make love. Sometimes we just lay in each other's arms. At times she was like a little girl, and it was hard to believe that this was the same domineering woman who'd ordered me to her room like a galley slave. We talked about me and my family and what I'd done the last couple of months. I found myself being completely open with her. I even told her about Mary Lou and how much I missed her. It was almost as if she'd adopted me. She said it was too bad about the way things had ended with Mary Lou. From what I had told her she said she thought that Mary Lou might have been the person with whom I could find myself. The idea of finding myself sounded melodramatic. I used to search for truth; now I'm searching for myself. "Search" seemed to me a corny word unless you were searching for your tent in a rainstorm or searching for your trousers in order to flee an irate husband. Come to think of it, Mona was the first married woman I'd ever made love to, other than Gloria, of course.

Whenever I tried to talk about Mrs. Huntington, Mona froze and the Texas despot warned me away. Soon I stopped trying to learn anything about Mrs. Randolph Huntington. To me she was just Mona, and she had no life outside Suite 507. I asked her out to have dinner with me, but she always refused. Several times we had dinner sent up. I never saw her again outside her suite.

Our afternoon meetings went on for almost a month, during which time I'd moved out of the Fairmont and taken a small, furnished second-story apartment on Polk Street. From the window of the bathroom I could see the

Golden Gate Bridge. It's how I always imagined it would be to live in San Francisco, at least while I was taking a leak. The people in San Francisco seemed friendly, but I never got to know anyone other than a few waiters at Fisherman's Wharf and Ghirardelli Square and the cashier at the City Lights Bookstore to whom my face became familiar. "How are you today?" and a few words about the weather was as far as it went. The weather was fairly constant, cool, partly sunny, a little fog, and rain maybe once a week, but even the consistency was something to talk about. The fishing boats at the wharf became familiar shapes and names; Little Josie, Dominic's Pride, The Good Hook, Santa Lucia, El Tiburon. I visited the Maritime Museum and the restored square riggers at Aquatic Park several times. I reread *Moby Dick* and traced the geography of the Pequod on the clipper in the harbor as closely as I could. I took the ferry to Sausalito, Tiburon, and Angel Island. I walked up Telegraph Hill and climbed Coit Tower. I did what any tourist would do. I walked through North Beach and saw Carol Doda's silicone-stuffed mammary glands at El Condor and Barnaby Conrad while I was having lunch at Enrico's. I'm pretty sure it was Barnaby Conrad. I'd read a lot of bullfighting books when I was in high school or, more properly, *libros de la corrida de toros.* I suppose I'd been infected partly through the mystique of Hemingway, but mostly through Conrad's tragic or maybe slightly maudlin account of the death of Manolete in Linares, Spain, 1947. It was a long time ago, and I can't remember if it was maudlin, but at the time it was effective, and Manolete became my boyhood idol along with, of course, Billy Vukovich.

I did a lot of reading in the mornings and tried to write, but nothing worked out. I started a few poems, but they were always poems I wanted to write, rather than poems that had to be written, and they went flat or sounded forced. They were forced. I felt melancholy and poetic. Why couldn't I write any poems?

It was early April when I found the envelope taped to Mona's door. She hadn't given any indication that she might be leaving, but then she rarely gave any indication of anything but a quiet listening interest in me. I opened the envelope and read the note written in her clear, open hand:

Dear Larry;

You're a lovely young man and I hope you find what you're looking for. There's a lot of good in you. Please don't give up on yourself. I'm sorry I had to end it this way.

Love,
Mona

23

I got very drunk that night and woke up the next morning feeling fine. I got dressed, made some coffee, and packed some bread, cheese, and a can of ginger ale in a brown paper bag. It was a clear day and warm for San Francisco. I drove past the Presidio and across the Golden Gate Bridge. In the month I'd lived in San Francisco this was the first time I'd driven over the bridge. I hadn't even crossed the Bay Bridge to see Berkeley. I took Highway 1 and the cutoff for the drive up Mount Tamalpais. I parked in the lot at the end of the road and looked out at the city. I heard a soothing voice chanting and discovered I was parked next to a Ford Econoline van with a large side door open. The chanting was coming from within the van. It was a pleasant voice and had an hypnotic effect similar to that I'd experienced in the fifth grade when Miss Crump leaned over me, resting her breasts on my shoulder to help me with my arithmetic. It wasn't much help, but it had been pleasant, the warmth on my shoulder, her perfume or bath powder swirling around my head. I had a recurring fantasy in which Miss Crump dragged me off, undressed me, gave me a bath, and tucked me in bed. Maybe I was a late bloomer, but at ten that was my idea of erotica. I think it was really the Miss Crump fantasy that Mona had brought to fruition.

I moved to where I could see into the van and discovered the voice was coming from a girl of about twenty wearing a white robe. She was sitting in a yoga position, reading to three or four small children. The inside of the van was painted black, and there were iridescent posters on the walls and incense burning in a bowl in the middle of the floor. It was a touching scene. There must be some religious significance to the parking lot at Mount Tamalpais. The young voice droned on until I'd moved close enough to see the cover on the book. There was a picture of a man disguised as the corpse of Rudolph Valentino, and I strained to make out the words "Kahlil Gibran." The whole scene plummeted to the basement of a Sausalito boutique. The voice lost its hypnotic quality.

"May I help you?" the girl said.

"What?" I said, realizing for the first time that I was standing full in the open door of the van and probably blocking her only source of reading light.

"Do you like Kahlil Gibran?" she asked.

"No," I said. "I think he's the rancid creation of sex-crazed teeny-boppers looking for instant mysticism, but I love you. Please go on. I could listen to you read the telephone book."

"Oh," she shrieked, "we can't escape the Philistines even here." The door slammed shut, almost taking my nose with it. Why couldn't I be civil?

I climbed through loose rocks to the top of the mountain and looked down on San Francisco. There was a light fog rolling under the bridge and a few white sails on the bay. I could see Berkeley, and to the north the green hills faded in the haze or met the ocean, I couldn't tell which. I climbed down to the car and drove down the mountain to the first scenic-view parking lot. I crossed the road and walked through the lush grass and spring flowers. I'm not good on the names of flowers, but they were colored like the crocuses that would be blooming in the last traces of snow back home. I laughed to myself at my still calling it home. I'd been gone almost the entire winter, and now a season was changing there without me. Maybe they didn't think of me anymore. Maybe Gloria had begun divorce proceedings or had me declared legally insane. No, she couldn't do that. I imagined myself returning to Brainard and people scratching their heads, saying, "Say, didn't you used to live around here? I could swear I've seen you before."

I opened the can of ginger ale and ate my bread and cheese. I listened to the wind hiss through the eucalyptus trees on the hill across the road and watched the fog roll over the hills from the sea. It was getting heavier, and the day was turning gray. Two motorcycles with ape-hanger handlebars and extended front forks roared up the road toward the top of the mountain. Below me on the hill a couple was wading through the grass holding a small child between them. A dog bounded through the grass ahead of them, and the man whistled and called to the dog.

I drove up to Drake's Bay, and the sky was completely overcast. I walked a long way down the beach. The sand was packed hard with moisture and slabs of brown rock protruded through the sand. They matched the brown of the cliffs above me. I looked up at the cliffs and thought how easily they could fall on me. I thought I could hear sea lions bark beyond the roar of the surf, but I wasn't sure. I remembered a poem by Frost about people looking out at the sea all day and not being able to see anything or even see into the water but watching it all day just the same. I walked a long way, but I was going nowhere. The beach was endless and I felt useless. I reflected that I hadn't done one thing in my life worthy of note. I'd left or been left by every woman I cared for. I certainly wasn't much of a father. I stopped and looked down at my hands, the long fingers, the veins and tendons showing through. They were attractive hands, maybe even classic hands, but useless. If I could make something with my hands, I thought. The line ran through my mind again. Maybe I've started another poem, I thought. Why couldn't I build a useful piece of furniture or put together a farm?

I walked back to the parking area and bought a cup of chicken soup from the vending machine in the park service building. It tasted pretty good for vending-machine soup but was almost too hot to hold in my hands. I set it down between sips and looked out the window at the gray sea.

I was alone on the beach, and I walked into the grass beside the building to take a leak. There were rest rooms in the building, but it had been a long time since I'd been able to piss outdoors. I noticed a jellylike green mass about the size of my fist undulating in the grass. At first I was repelled, but then I realized it was a slug, a giant snail without a shell, a member of the mollusk family. That was about all I remembered from biology. I bent close to the ground and noticed some small black bugs nibbling the edge of a blade of grass. It started to rain. I zipped up my fly and ran for the car.

It was dark. I stopped for dinner at a little restaurant near San Anselmo and had chicken curry. The waitress was tall and homely. She wore a muslin blouse and a floor-length wool skirt. I wanted her, but I was polite and contained myself.

Visibility was poor in the rain, and the twisting, unfamiliar road made driving difficult. I was cold and turned on the heater. If I could make something with my hands, I thought again. No, if I made something with my hands, a farm, a mollusk, a moonship. The words just followed. I didn't know where they'd come from, but they were there. I wanted to stop and write them down, but I didn't have any paper. I said them again and again so I wouldn't forget them, then tried not to think about it anymore.

I parked the car and ran up the stairs to my apartment. I switched on the lamp in the center of the kitchen table and got my pen and a tablet of lined paper. I quickly wrote down the two lines but was distracted by the shadow from my hand that the single lamp cast on the wall. "A lamp to light these walls," the third line. It began to flow:

> *If I made something with my hands*
> *a farm a mollusk a moonship*
> *a lamp to light these walls*
> *these idle hands*
> *something made to leave behind*
> *the chiseled head of a god*
> *any god*
> *that you might imagine his hooded eyes*
> *a window*
> *to frame your desire*
> *or contain your discontent*
>
> *Already there are holes in the leaves*
> *the edge of newness worn off*
> *green darkens to summer*
>
> *I imagine my hands the hands of a sculptor*
> *pictured in the book of palmistry*
> *veins pulsing through*
> *tendons clear*
> *hands to be severed and preserved*

reaching into the earth
for stones roots coal or black water

I was elated. I'd finally written a poem. It was too new for me to know if it were any good, but it was good enough to give me that total exhilaration that only comes from writing a poem. I put the tablet in the drawer with the spoons, put it there to incubate until I could half forget it was mine and then decide if it were good. I took a long walk to the wharf and along the waterfront. It was raining hard, but I didn't care. I loved the rain.

PART 4

By the time I'd decided that the poem was good, I'd
bought plane tickets to Paris with a stopover in London.
"I'm a poet," I said to myself. I had an identity, at least
for a while. I spent the next few days closing up the
apartment and selling the Porsche. I got five thousand
dollars from an imported car dealer, put two thousand of
it in traveler's checks, and deposited the rest in a savings
account at the Bank of America, for contingencies. I
bought a double-knit beige suit, some new drip-dry shirts,
and even a couple of neckties and packed them along with
a pair of Levi's in a nylon bag. My last day in San Francisco I typed fifteen copies of the poem and sent them to
fifteen different magazines—*The New Yorker, Harper's, The
Nation, The Atlantic, The Saturday Review,* and ten little
magazines selected at random from the periodicals section
of the San Francisco Public Library. I enclosed stamped,
self-addressed envelopes with my soon-to-be-no-longer
Polk Street address and fed them into the mail slot one
by one. The Mystery Poet. I had a vision of the checks,
rejections, and letters of acceptance piling up behind the
front door of the empty apartment and of the editors of
all those magazines reading my poem in each other's pages

and arranging to meet for lunch at Le Côte Basque to "discuss this embarrassing situation."

What if someone really took it? I thought. I took one last ride on the Angel Island-Sausalito ferry, one last ride on the Powell Street cable car, and one last meal of Dungeness crab at Tarantino's. I dreamed of London and Paris while I picked the delicate white meat from the shells and watched the fishing boats bobbing at the wharf. Parisians were harsh and arrogant with foreigners who spoke imperfect French, but I spoke almost no French. I'd read an interview with the French actor, Jean Louis Trintignant, in which he said that he thought timidity was a form of arrogance because the timid person believed everyone was watching him, their thoughts occupied with what he did. It was a revelation to me. I would not be timid I decided, and I would speak no French. I'll make them meet me on my turf with their imperfect English, I thought, and ordered another half-bottle of Chablis with which to savor the last of the crab.

My plane to New York was due to leave at 10:07 the following morning, and I called the cab company and arranged for a taxi to pick me up at 8:30. I laid out my clothes, my passport, my health certificate, my money belt, and my traveler's checks. It was like preparing for an operation or outfitting an expedition. I'd been to London once before, when I was seventeen, but I'd been alone and miserable. Perhaps I was too young to appreciate it, I thought. I'm sure it'll be different this time.

I went to bed at 10, but I couldn't sleep and switched on "The Dick Cavett Show" to watch Gore Vidal and Norman Mailer tear each other apart while Cavett and Janet Flanner tried futilely to cool it. I pulled the covers over my head, horrified at the fangs and enraged inarticulation that emerged from behind the dust-jacket images of these literary personages. I was grateful for books and decided I didn't ever really want to meet any writers in person. It was good to be snug in my rented bed. I was overwhelmed with the security of being a disinterested third party and drifted off to sleep. In my dreams I invited Dick Cavett and Janet Flanner into my inner circle of friends, all well-behaved and civil. I was the only one who didn't fit.

The taxi was there on time, in fact a few minutes early. I dropped the key in the mailbox for the landlord and slammed the door on Polk Street. On the ride to the airport the driver told me about all San Francisco's hotspots, which ones are gyps and which ones have "real action." Why is it you always run into the cabbie with all the hot tips when you're leaving town? I gave him a generous tip and told him I'd keep all his suggestions for my next trip to "the Bay Area." I told him I was a word salesman and left him to speculate on what that meant.

I had a mushroom omelet with champagne, a few chapters of *The Tropic of Cancer*, which I'd bought along as a primer for Paris, a rancid movie about love and death at Harvard, and a short nap on the flight to New York. I looked out the window and saw America below me, stretching to the horizon under a broken layer of stratus clouds. The Santa Fe Trail's down there, I thought through a champagne haze, and Donner Pass and the Holiday Inn in Des Moines. I wondered how many times they'd changed the sheets since Mary Lou and I slept there and how long the aura of a person lingered in a room after he'd left and if it were different for different rooms and different people.

I had a three-hour layover at Kennedy during which I explored the TWA terminal, had a steak dinner I didn't really feel like eating, and sipped sherry in the bar, watching people, eavesdropping on conversations, and making up stories about myself. I decided that if anyone asked, I was traveling on business I wasn't permitted to discuss. That's what I told the girl who sat across the aisle on the flight to London. After takeoff I managed to move to the seat next to her. She was mostly purple, a purple chemise, purple eye makeup, purple hose. Sensuous. I took her to be a woman of the world. She had a sibylline ambience, but it turned out that she was twenty-one, from Grand Rapids, Michigan, and on her way to join her husband, who was a sergeant based in Turkey. The night was short, whistling toward the sun at 600 miles per hour. We landed in Amsterdam at dawn. London was fogged in, and we had to wait for it to clear. I wrote postcards to Ozzie Pierce and Tom Kalab with no explanation of what I was doing in the Netherlands. The purple girl, whose name turned out to be Joan, held my hand while we drank. She told me about her plans to sabotage the army and about all the trouble she'd caused while her husband was based at Fort Dix. I asked her if she didn't think it was dangerous telling me. She laughed and ran her fingers over my wrist. She said she could smell a pig and that I was definitely cool. I'm sure my hair, which by that time had grown well over my collar, reassured her. She got a continuing flight to Rome, and I was alone with Henry Miller in a strange land.

25

In the surreal climate of San Francisco I'd almost forgotten it was spring in the world. It was cool in London, but there were birds singing, crocuses, and daffodils, and the sky had that Gainsborough look. It was late afternoon, and I told the cab driver to take me to the Westbury Hotel. I thought of Rex Harrison and Audrey Hepburn on the ride into town and wondered if Henry Higgins might have lived in one of the still elegant white Victorian houses we passed on Kensington. The clerk at the hotel desk was young, unused to his striped trousers and cutaway coat. He felt obliged to assume what he assumed to be the manners of those he assumed to be his betters. He flitted about and made a great fuss over the fact that they'd been overbooked, but finally managed to "ferret out a room." He somehow looked like a ferret. The one thing I'd remembered about the Westbury was a one-armed elevator operator who'd lit my cigarette with a match when I couldn't get my lighter to work. He could pull a box of matches from his pocket, open it, remove a match, and strike it with one hand faster than I could with two. Apart from my encounter with the friendly prostitute, it was my clearest memory of London at seventeen.

The porter motioned for me to enter the elevator, and I heard a voice say, "Hello, there. We haven't seen you for some time." As I lifted my eyes from the elevator floor, the first thing I saw was an empty sleeve and then that face that reminded me of the face of an Italian prizefighter I'd seen in movies about gangsters and waterfront warlords.

"You," I said. "You remember me?"

"Yes, sir. Of course you've filled out a bit. You was just a skinny kid last time you was here."

"That's incredible." I felt I'd met an old friend. It started coming back to me. "I think I remember your telling me you used to live in New York," I said.

"That's right, sir, Brooklyn. That's very good."

We'd reached my floor, and at that moment I felt at home in London and wished I'd planned to stay longer.

"Well, see you later," I said, as the elevator doors slid shut. I'm not sure, but I think the porter was sneering at my familiarity. But it seemed a quaint sneer, simply what tradition expected, without the latent intimidating hostility one felt in a New York bellhop. I'd caught that same quaint sneer on the face of the immigration officer who'd checked my passport at Heathrow.

"Are you on business or pleasure?" he'd asked.

"Business."

"What is the nature of your business?"

"Exploration."

"What sort of exploration?"

"The esculent possibilities of the human universe." I'd had a lot of sherry on the plane. He inhaled sharply through his nose and stamped my passport with a punishing thump.

I hadn't eaten since breakfast somewhere over Belgium.

I called room service and ordered a mixed grill, creamed spinach, coffee, a chocolate éclair, and a *London Times*. I took a long shower and greeted the waiter wrapped in a towel, improper, I'm sure, but convenient. My mother used to urge me to pack a bathrobe for just this sort of situation and tried to buy me some pajamas when I'd married Gloria. "Nothing is so shocking to a young bride as the sight of a naked man," she said. But Gloria hadn't been shocked by the sight of a naked man before we were married, so I felt safe in assuming that she wouldn't be shocked after the ceremony.

The mixed grill was delicious, particularly the lamb and sausages. The sausages were simply better than the sausages at home. Someday I may take up residency in England just for the sausages. I glanced at the paper and saw unfamiliar headlines that looked almost fictitious. The Home Secretary was issuing distressing statistics.

"Dear me," I said in my best imitation of an Oxford accent and folded the paper. I got dressed, cashed a traveler's check at the desk, and walked down Regent Street to Piccadilly Circus. The English bills were larger and seemed substantial rubbing against my thigh, but I couldn't believe they were real money, and I rarely considered the price of anything.

London was crisp. Even the neon of Piccadilly Circus seemed more colorful than commercial, probably because the names were unfamiliar: Rothhams, Players, Guinness, Vauxhall, Coca-Cola. Well, scratch Coca-Cola. I walked down Shaftsbury and went to a movie at the Palace Theatre on Cambridge Circus. I loved the names. I held out a handful of money and asked the girl at the box office to take what she needed. It was a Bergman film about adultery. On the walk back to the hotel, London began to look like any other city. The faces in the neon glare of Piccadilly seemed grotesque, as if seen in a funhouse mirror. Jet lag had caught up with me.

It was raining in the morning, but I was determined to make good on my one full day in London. I bought an airmail stamp from the concierge, a Wordsworth commemorative, and he told me my reservation in Paris was confirmed at the Hotel Lotti. I thanked him and gave him a tenpence tip.

I took a taxi to the Tower of London and lingered by the small stone monument and brass plaque which marked the site of the private scaffold where Lady Jane Grey and five others, including Anne Boleyn and the Earl of Essex, had lost their heads. I listened to the Beefeater dramatize the story and felt chills and an almost overwhelming melancholy. My whole life seemed to be coming to this place, four centuries too late to rescue Lady Jane. I've always been able to imagine time travel and therefore believe in its feasibility. But in all of my fantasized voyages to Elizabethan England, I'm arrested for my outlandish clothes and end by desperately and futilely trying to explain to them that I'm an American. When I meet Shakespeare, he's a very bland man, consumed in writing and producing plays and unaware of his reputation. I try to convince him how much he will someday mean to the world, and he says he likes my wit and offers me the part of the fool in *King Lear*. I take it, but I'm not well received. . . .

At Westminster Abbey I fought my way through the hordes of tourists regurgitated by the buses parked in front. A guide was speaking in German. I thought of Gunther the Terrible and felt the smug satisfaction of having an ocean between us. Still, it had been a good lucky punch, and the story could no doubt be improved. I finally made it to the Poet's Corner and lingered over the stone marked T. S. Eliot. "Well, Tom, it's April," I said to myself, "and I feel like a pair of ragged claws." I tried to imagine the smell of steaks in passageways and walking on the beach in white flannel trousers rolled up to the knee, eating a peach, the juice running down my infirm chin and spoiling my dickie. I wanted to be buried in Westminster Abbey, but the only American who'd gotten recognition here, besides the turncoat Eliot, was Longfellow, who'd paddled his way into Victorian hearts in a birchbark canoe. Thomas Hardy was buried here, though his heart had been removed and buried in Dorset. I mused over writing an epic poem about Thomas Hardy's heart trying to get back into his body. Of course, there would be technical difficulties. The heart would have to sneak into the Abbey at night. A heart traveling by itself in broad daylight is certain to attract attention. In New York they'd just write it off as the residue from another mugging, but Londoners weren't quite so jaded. "The Surreptitious Journey of Thomas Hardy's Heart." I wondered if *The New Yorker* would publish it? They might if I threw in a few oblique references to Brooks Brothers and Bergdorf-Goodman. I noticed a carved stone high on the wall that read, "O Rare Ben Jonson" and imagined one beside it, "Too Much Larry Bancroft." It was time to leave. Where had they buried Richard Burton?

I went to the National Portrait Gallery on Trafalgar Square and bought copious postcard pictures of poets: a businesslike Blake, a dreamy Keats, Byron hamming it up in a turban. I speculated that if he were alive today he'd wear a purple T-shirt that said "Club Mandible" in gold letters with his penname, "Capitan Berserko" on the pocket. Lord Gordon George Berserko. There was a young Coleridge, who looked teary as if someone had stolen his jackknife, a wispy young Hopkins, a frazzled Yeats and, of course, the now heartless Hardy. Maybe it would be his body that would try to rejoin his heart. I'd have to consider that. Rod Serling might buy it.

I went to Carnaby Street and bought some outrageous psychedelic shirts. I had lunch at the Cheshire Cheese in Fleet Street and met two three-named lady poetesses who claimed to be descendants of Mallory. They were furious about the invasion of Hastings and were mounting a campaign to remove all Norman influences from the English language. I told them I sold insurance and paid my bill. As I was leaving I suggested they also endeavor to remove all Saxon influences and try to reestablish pure Cro-Magnon. "All our problems are a matter of language," I said. "A rose by any other name might be a tit."

"How quaint," I heard the older one say, as I turned and fled.

I walked down Temple Lane and along the Victoria Embankment. The rain had stopped, and the sun was trying to burn through. There were a few tugs pulling barges on the Thames and a lot of little blue-and-white-hulled boats that looked like toys. I crossed the river at Waterloo Bridge. The Houses of Parliament across the river looked as if they were dressed in camouflage. The soot had been washed away in spots, and the sun cast shadows in all the pockets and crevices of the intricate stonework. I looked at Big Ben. This is how I imagined it would be to live in London. It was always late afternoon in November. The sun was streaming low over the Thames, half hiding behind Big Ben, who was sounding five o'clock to tell me it was time for me to scamper home so my Nannie could give me a bath and dress me in my snuggies. I'd probably gotten the impression as a child reading *Mary Poppins* or *Peter Pan,* and it had stuck. Why not? I could hire a Nannie who would bathe me. It would be very secure. It might be a lot of fun.

I walked out on Westminster Bridge and looked down at the murky Thames flowing beneath me. I tried to imagine Joseph Conrad leaving this river for the Congo, his final sight of London as he drifted to the sea. I watched my shadow on the water and then on the stone of the bridge. It didn't really look like a gunfighter's shadow now. In my trench coat it was more like foreign intrigue, and I tried to imagine zither music. But there wasn't any music, only the noise of traffic and a jet overhead on its final approach to Heathrow. It all seemed so familiar, as if I'd been there a hundred times before, the angle of sunlight through the clouds, my shadow on the bridge, the distant barges. I probably had been there before, when I was seventeen. It was the picture of London I carried in my head. I wondered how many undiscovered places I'd feel at home in? Maybe if I went home it would be different now. Maybe I'd see it clearly for the first time and solutions would be evident. Maybe I should have Gloria come to London, away from everything that had come between us. Maybe I should try to find Mary Lou and bring her here. Maybe I should get them both together. Maybe I'm crazy, I thought.

I walked up Whitehall to Trafalgar Square. The square was jammed with people. It was a rally of some sort; there were red banners with hammers and sickles, black banners with swastikas, crosses, peace symbols, and clenched fists. I watched for a while from the edge of the crowd and tried to decide if the Young Fascists were trying to disrupt a Young Communist rally, or if the Young Christians were trying to disrupt them both, or if the police were trying to disrupt them all, or if they were all trying to disrupt a demonstration by the Fraternal Order of Police, if they have such a thing in England. It all had a mildly comic air about it until a band of skinheads, boys with shaved heads, big boots, and suspenders, began beating longhairs at random on the edge of the crowd. The police tried to intervene, but the crowd was too thick, and bloody skulls began to drip on the Strand. London lost its quaint charm. I felt a nausea welling up in the pit of my stomach. I dragged one of the longhairs into a doorway so he wouldn't be trampled. He was bleeding from somewhere under his hair, and I think he had a broken nose. I grabbed a bobby by the sleeve and led him to the fallen man. He said he'd take care of it and told me to move on.

I walked back to Westbury but couldn't go in. I walked on to Berkeley Square and sat on a bench. In the center of the square a man and a woman were kissing as if they were alone. I was getting cold and walked back to the hotel. The doorman tipped his hat and said, "Did you have a nice day, sir?" I tried to answer, but I didn't have any words.

I ran a hot bath and ordered three double gin-and-tonics. I soaked in the tub and drank gin. I felt sick to my stomach and thought about vomiting, but I turned on the television and fell asleep watching a "Peyton Place" rerun.

26

I woke up about six o'clock, called room service, and had a chicken sandwich and some coffee sent up. I tried to read *The Tropic of Cancer* but after two hours began to get stir-crazy. I couldn't stay locked up in my room with the memories of Trafalgar Square. I had to talk to someone. I got dressed, went down to the street, and hailed a taxi. I asked the driver where the action was, and he recommended a club on Bond Street. " 'Course one of them birds may charge you thirty quid. Coo-ee. It's awful, ain't it. 'Course you try something for under ten, and you're likely to wake up with a sort of nasty discharge."

"No discharge, thanks," I said, and he let me out in front of the club. It was a private club, but for two pounds I was able to join at the door. I was led into a large, dimly lighted room that looked like a movie set nightclub. The host seated me at a table near the stage and asked if I'd like to have company.

"Why not?" I said.

It was as if it were all happening to somebody else, a film of the country boy come to the wicked city. *The Rube.* The waiter returned with a girl, and The Rube rose and seated her. The band was playing "Red Roses for a

Blue Lady," and the speakers were directly overhead.

"What's your name?" The Rube shouted.

"Georgette," said the girl. The Rube was struck by how much Georgette resembled another girl he'd known recently, a bit more pudgy perhaps, but the long blonde hair and the eyes. Her voice was definitely crisp. The Rube was excited. He'd never really been in an intimate or semi-intimate situation with a girl who had a British accent. He found accents erotic and wanted to collect them, a catalogue of whispers in his ear: British, southern United States, French, of course, lisping Castilian Spanish, deep-throated, soft Italian, nasal Russian heavy on the "V's," delicate and fluttering Japanese, perhaps even Chinese, though he didn't know how that would differ from Japanese. He began to realize how large the world was. A map stretched before him like an endless menu.

Conversation was difficult because of the band, but that was just as well. It gave The Rube time to collect his thoughts, to determine just where to begin.

"Would you like a drink?" he asked.

"Yes, I'd like a bottle of champagne," Georgette said.

"A whole bottle?"

"It does come in bottles, doesn't it?"

"Oh, yes, of course. Waiter, a bottle of champagne for the lady." How easy it was once he got started. "Where are you from?" he asked.

"London," she replied, in a "where else" tone of voice.

"Born here?"

"No, but I live here now. I was born in Blackpool."

"That's a resort, isn't it?"

"Yes, you know, beaches and all that."

"Oh, yes, on the ocean." The Rube was pleased. They were getting on famously.

"What state are you from?" Georgette asked.

"Michigan."

"Do you travel a lot?" Now they were talking about him. He didn't feel quite so lonely anymore. There were prospects of a real friendship forming. The waiter brought the champagne and displayed the label, though The Rube couldn't see it in the dim light.

"Fine," he said, with an approving wave of his hand. The waiter popped the cork and poured a glass for Georgette. She opened her purse and took out a swizzle stick.

"You drink a lot of champagne?" The Rube asked.

"Yes, quite a lot, but I can't stand the bubbles."

"I bet they'd give you a lot of gas in the long run." That wasn't exactly what he'd wanted to say. He ordered a gin-and-tonic and smiled at Georgette. Georgette smiled at him. He decided that she didn't really look like a professional.

"Could we go somewhere later?" he asked.

"It'll be a hundred dollars," she said.

"Oh, of course. That's quite reasonable."

"Could I have a sandwich, please? I'm a bit peckish."

"Of course. Waiter, could we have a sandwich for the lady." The waiter disappeared before The Rube could tell him what kind of sandwich, or before he could even ask Georgette what kind of a sandwich she wanted. There must be a standard sandwich, he thought.

The floor show had begun. Two darling men with permanent glucose smiles dancing among half-dressed chorus girls to the tune of "Lullaby of Broadway." This didn't quite fit his conception of London: Margaret Rutherford as the witty duchess who'd survived the blitz, J. Alfred Prufrock in his rich, modest tie asserted with a simple pin, carrying an umbrella and wearing a bowler on his way to measuring out another day in coffee spoons —or was it teaspoons? The changing of the guard at Buckingham Palace, Big Ben, Rolls-Royce, and Parliament cigarettes. The girls danced off a few more of their feathers.

"Do you like the show?" Georgette asked.

"Yes, well, it's interesting."

"It's too bad you're here tonight, because one of the girls, the best really, well, she's a wonderful juggler, but she's sick in hospital.

"Oh, I'm sorry to hear that. Nothing serious, I hope." He tried to show concern by making lines in his forehead.

"No; well, it's her appendix frankly, and the only trouble is, it'll probably leave a scar. The patrons don't like to see scars on the dancing girls, so she may have to modify her costume. But on the other hand, I've known some patrons who really find scars quite attractive. Could I have another bottle of champagne, please?"

It seemed to The Rube that she'd gone through the champagne awfully fast and he suspected that it might have been a dummy bottle, but what the hell, he was being a sport. A wave of the hand brought another bottle of champagne and the nameless sandwich. The Rube felt a question welling up in his chest. He didn't really want to ask, but he felt a genuine concern for Georgette. They'd really begun to establish communication, to talk about important things, to become friends.

"Georgette, you're such a lovely girl. Don't you find it, ahh," he stumbled here looking for a word, "unpleasant, burdensome, having to go off somewhere with someone like me?" He really didn't want to add to the trials of her life.

"Well, we don't have to go if we don't want to. I really enjoy it a lot more than secretarial work. It pays better and I've got a little mouth at home to feed."

"Oh, I see." Now he felt better about the whole thing. He was helping to feed a little mouth. In these times of high unemployment and inflation, that was something.

"Besides," she said, "you get to meet a lot of interesting people."

A woman came to the table with a tray of artificial flowers and said, "Flowers for the lady?"

"All right, how much?"

"Two pounds."

He put two one-pound notes on the tray, a little shocked. The flower vendor thanked him and went away. "Boy, they really milk you for everything they can get here, don't they?"

"Well, you didn't have to buy it," Georgette said. The flower lay mockingly on the table among the falling ashes of her cigarette.

"Oh," said The Rube. He hadn't thought of that.

Georgette asked for and got another bottle of champagne and a package of cigarettes. The Rube kept drinking gin-and-tonic. Georgette told him about the dancing boys, how one of them was gay and how everybody loved him.

"Only one?" the Rube asked.

"Oh yes, Reggie's got a wife and seven little ones."

"Amazing."

She pointed out a man who had the evil, jaded look of a James Bond villain and said that he was a regular patron and a very good friend of the owner of the club. He smiled and nodded to Georgette and almost dropped his monocle. The Rube's thoughts flashed back to the Harum Scarum Club in Denver and Mary Lou laughing at the suckers. But this is different, Mary Lou, he thought, Georgette and I are friends and she's got a little mouth to feed. He pushed Mary Lou and her laughter out of his mind. Georgette told him all about her divorce and her moving to London. About her job as a secretary and then about finally finding her spot at the club, about her trips back to Blackpool, with the little mouth, to visit her parents. The Rube thought it was quite a touching story.

"What time can we leave?" he asked.

"Well, it's just midnight, and I don't get off until two, but if you talked to the headwaiter and slipped him a few pounds, he might let me off early." She pointed out the headwaiter, and The Rube slipped him a couple of pounds. The headwaiter said he thought it would be all right for Georgette to leave.

"What hotel are you staying at?" Georgette asked.

"The Westbury."

"Uh, uh, that's no good. I'll have to ask Michael to phone and see if he can get us a room somewhere else."

"What's wrong with the Westbury?"

"Very stuffy about that sort of thing."

"Oh."

Georgette motioned to Michael and mumbled something in his ear. About five minutes later Michael returned and mumbled something in Georgette's ear. She turned to The Rube and said, "It's all set, but be sure and give Michael something when we leave."

"Well, of course," said The Rube. He was a little irritated by Georgette's thinking she had to tell him what to do. He called for the check, which in the glare of the flashlight the waiter shined on it said forty pounds. The Rube swallowed hard and paid with the play money from his pocket. He also signed a $100 traveler's check.

"Don't forget the tip," Georgette said.

"It's all taken care of," he said with pinched lips.

They stumbled out through the dark club and into the comparatively bright entrance hall by the cloak room.

"I'll be with you in a minute," Georgette said, and trotted up the stairs. The Rube redeemed his trench coat and slipped Michael a one-pound note. Georgette returned.

"The Lady Georgette," Michael said, holding her coat for her.

"Good night, sir, have a pleasant evening."

"Good night," said The Rube, thinking to himself that they were really quite friendly.

"The Lady Georgette," the doorman said, "Your car?"

"Please, Donald," Georgette said.

The doorman walked down the street and returned driving one of those miniature British cars. The Rube didn't have to be told to tip him. The streets were wet, and a light fog hung in the air between the gray stone buildings of Bond Street.

Georgette drove very well, though it made him uncomfortable to be sitting on her left. She opened a tin box and offered him a mint. He wondered if this was standard procedure or if she were trying to tell him he had bad breath. Anyone could have bad breath, he decided.

The street looked familiar, and he realized it was Kennsington, almost deserted. Georgette wheeled the car into the courtyard of one of the houses The Rube had suspected of having belonged to Henry Higgins. The lobby was gloomy and deserted except for the cadaverous night porter, half-reclining behind the desk. The Rube signed the register "Mr. and Mrs. Ted Heath." "Ha, ha," he said to himself, but the porter didn't look at it.

"That'll be seven pounds," he said. The Rube paid. The porter picked up a large ring with a single key on it and led them to the elevator. The Rube noticed that he walked with a limp. They got out at the fifth floor and walked through a maze of twisting hallways. The porter opened the door and said, "I think this'll be adequate for all your little needs." He took the key with him and limped back down the hallway.

The room was plain and clean. The curtains were already drawn, and the only light came from the bathroom. The Rube looked at Georgette. She really looked quite sweet, smiling out from under her blonde bangs. Her sequined mesh sweater was bulging where her breasts were trussed up under it. He knew they were trussed up when she took the sweater off. Her bra presented them as if they were sweetbreads on a platter fastened to her chest.

I really ought to do something, The Rube thought. He went to her and kissed her. She took him in her arms and massaged his mouth and chin with her incredibly soft lips. She held the back of his head in her hands. Then she said, "Can I have my present now?"

"Your what?" he said softly.

"My present. You know," she said, winking.

"Oh, yes, your present." He opened his billfold and handed her a one-hundred-dollar bill. She kissed him, folded the bill, and put it in her purse. She began to undress. He began to undress, piling his clothes on top of the dresser.

"This ain't exactly the Ritz, is it," he said, trying to make conversation.

"No, but it's very nice and reasonable. You ought to stay here on your next trip to London." She was down to her bra and panties. "I'll be right back," she said, and went into the bathroom and closed the door. The Rube pulled down his shorts and lay them on top of the pile. He crawled in between the cool sheets and lay waiting. He heard the running water and wondered what exactly she was doing. He wished he could watch her. He thought that it would be easy for him to sneak out of bed and take the hundred dollars back while she was in the bathroom but dismissed the thought as unsportsmanlike. He wasn't lonely anymore, and he and Georgette were friends. She came back into the room. She was really quite pretty in the light from the bathroom. She got something from her purse and lay down beside him. "I've got a present for you," she said, and handed him a small plastic container about the size of an ice cube.

"What?" he said, not understanding.

"It's for you to put on," she whispered.

He had some difficulty opening the case and finally crushed it against the night stand by the bed. The condom was lubricated, and Georgette took it from his hand and rolled it down over his penis. He shuddered at her first touch. He kissed her, and she began rubbing her breasts against him. He dropped his head to her breast and kissed her nipples. He began massaging her clitoris, and she cradled his balls in her hand. Soon she pulled him onto her and guided him into place between her legs. She made a few moans, gyrated her hips, and it was over. He faded quickly and slipped out of her. He lay beside her for awhile, and she patted her belly and said she was getting fat. She pointed out the sunlamp lines on her breast and hips and said she liked to maintain her summer tan all year. He got out of bed and went into the bathroom. He pulled off the limp rubber and dropped it into the toilet. He wiped the remaining semen off with a piece of toilet paper and flushed it. He washed his hands and then stood studying his eyes in the mirror. There was a slow but constant drip of water from the ceiling. It spattered on the edge of the tub.

They kissed in the parking lot before he got into his cab. He thought he should kiss her to make it more like a lover's parting, but it really felt like the formal handshake that concludes a business deal. "The Westbury" was all he said to the driver. The fog was about the same.

27

I took a shower and lay on the bed. I stared at the ceiling and tried to remember Georgette's face. I couldn't. She had long blonde hair, a little mouth to feed, and that was all. I'm sure she didn't even remember my name. Had I even told her my name? I was like a report she might have typed when she was a secretary, a day's work, done and forgotten. I totaled up the evening's expenses and they came to two hundred and forty-three dollars and change. I laughed out loud, laughed at The Rube, who'd acted just like all the lonely traveling salesmen and conventioneers he'd scorned in the past. He'd bought an illusion of love that was no illusion at all. He might as well have whacked off. I thought I could hear Mary Lou laughing. We were laughing together. Then she stopped and looked at me. "What about us, Larry?" she said. "What about your wife? We can't spend the rest of our lives running away."

"I'm not running away," I said. "I'm not running away. I'm not, I'm not, I'm not, I'm not." It trailed away like an echo.

I sat up in bed. I'd been asleep. The lights of the city were reflected off the fog outside my window, making the sky a crepuscular gray. "I'm not running away," I thought. I thought of men I'd known who talked too much about being happy, loving their wives or liking their jobs, as if they were trying to convince themselves.

"Happiness is wanting what you have, not having what you want," my father said again.

I'd seen myself shot in Algiers. Because my life had fallen to aimless wandering and I had nowhere else to go, I eventually went to Algiers, and having no excuse for being there that was plausible to the pragmatic Algerian secret police, it was assumed I was a spy for some undetermined power. I was summarily stood against a *café-au-lait* stucco wall, already variegated and ventilated with small granoblastic punctures I could palpate with the fingertips of my hands, which were tied behind me, and in the penumbra of the desert evening was shot by fifteen unsanitary bolt-action Enfields pilfered from the original filming of *Beau Geste*. I've got to stop somewhere, I thought, somewhere short of Algiers. The word "confrontation" haunted me, as did "relevance," "viable," and "solution." "Face facts," my father barked. I saw a dark street in Phoenix again, one I had to make myself walk down. My analeptic firehose demanded I clean up my life.

I was going to Paris. I'd try to face facts in Paris, I decided—it was neutral ground—face Gloria and Mary Lou in Paris. Maybe it wasn't really a crazy idea. I'd always had a notion that exotic places could defuse the intrusion of reality. Why else did they hold peace talks in Paris, summit conferences in Yalta and Honolulu?

I wired Gloria. I asked her to meet me in Paris. "No tricks this time. I'll be there. I want to get things straight between us." I wired Mary Lou in care of the Silver Cloud Bar in Benton Harbor. It was the only address I had. I wired air fare and asked her to come. "I'm sorry. I'm ready to talk about us."

I needed an aide-de-camp, a counselor, and a bodyguard. It was easier to walk down a dark street if you had confident company. I wired Tom Kalab:

Money wired separately.
If you can, come to Paris.
Summit meeting planned. Need support.
They say it's a lovely place.
R.S.V.P.

Larry Bancroft
Hotel Loti
8 Rue Castiglone
Paris

I wrote a note to myself to make additional hotel reservations in the morning. I settled back on the bed and basked in the glow of my resolution. It was similar to the way I felt after paying my income tax. I thought about The Rube again and laughed. It all seemed so far away.

I drifted off to sleep and dreamed of the chuang-yin my grandfather had brought back from China. She was almost life-size and stood among the cedar trees in his backyard. In time the cedars grew so thick I had to push my way through the branches to find her. She could have been a statue of a madonna without child except for the eyefolds. As a child I used to go to her on summer evenings in the premature dark of the cedar grove and tell her I loved her. I told her all my problems and seemed to come away feeling better. I was afraid my grandfather had forgotten her. He'd gone to China after my grandmother had been killed in an auto accident. He went to scatter her ashes in the Pacific and to try to forget, and he came home with the chuang-yin. I was carving a miniature of the woman for him when he died. It wasn't coming out right. I wasn't much of a carver, but I didn't want him to forget her. The last time I saw him he was sitting at his dinner table holding a finch that had dazed itself flying into the picture window. The bird's head was all I could see emerging from his fist. He was stroking it with his index finger. He looked at the carving and told me I was trying too hard to copy the chuang-yin in the cedar grove, that I'd have to put more of myself into it. "You're carving your idea of what a statue should be." He went to the window and opened his fist. He knew the bird was ready. It sat on his palm a moment, looked around, and then flew into the dusk. He closed the window and started up the stairs. In the morning he was dead.

I woke up feeling better, called room service, and ordered scrambled eggs, sausages, and coffee. I sat at the table and looked out the window. It had been almost three months since I left home. It had been thirty years since I'd left the womb, and all I had to show for it were a few poems. I'd lived the life everyone expected of me for all but three months, and what was the difference? "I am a poet," I said to myself. "I am." I drank another cup of coffee and looked out again at the soft gray sky. I tried to imagine Gloria in Paris, but the picture I got was of Mary Lou. Everything I imagined saying to Gloria, I was saying to Mary Lou. I hoped that when they were together I'd be able to tell them apart.

The flight from London was short and smooth. The one-armed elevator operator was sorry to see me go. As I rode to the airport I thought about the riot in Trafalgar. I wondered if the man I'd dragged from the crowd had recovered. I noticed a bloodstain on the sleeve of my coat.

28

Paris was almost too beautiful to be trusted. Henry Miller had called her a beautiful whore who leaves you dissatisfied, but I think of her as a glamorous wife who has, perhaps, a few designs of her own. In the spring light, she was not crisp like London, but amber and dulcet. Maybe it was simply that there was more smog, but if it was smog, God bless smog. God bless all the illusions in my romantic soul. In Paris you could piss on my leg and tell me it was raining. I wouldn't care.

Three messages were waiting at the Hotel Loti when I checked in. All acceptances, Gloria's tainted with admonitions of the absurd.

I could see the Place Vendôme from my window, a double-opening full-length window with a wrought-iron railing. It was almost a balcony. In the other direction, the Jardin des Tuileries. Almost like Central Park, I thought. I walked to the Place de la Concorde, and on the horizon I could just make out the Eiffel Tower. Yes, by God, I was in Paris. I'd recognize it anywhere. I walked up the Champs Élysées and could see the Arc de Triomphe looming over it. I pinched myself and almost started skipping. I was in Paris. I thought of those Gene Kelly and Fred Astaire movies where they danced through the streets and walk halfway up the walls of the Seine embankment. I'd always felt silly watching them. On the Champs, no one seemed to be in a hurry. That is, none of the pedestrians seemed to be in a hurry. The cars were all traveling at racing speed. I watched numerous near-misses and felt my old wounds smart. People strolled on the sidewalks with coats over their arms or around their shoulders. It was easy to spot the American tourists, and I hoped I wasn't obvious. I knew I would be when I opened my mouth. "Un café, s'il vous plaît," I said to the waiter at a sidewalk cafe, expecting him to sneer. But he didn't. He merely nodded as if he understood and brought me coffee. It worked. It was easy. I could live in Paris. At least I could be sure of having my coffee. Where were the haughty French? The coffee was good, and I ordered another cup. I said, "L'addition, s'il vous plaît," and the waiter left the check on the table. I figured it out with the help of my guidebook and left a two-franc tip. The waiter picked up the coins and said, "Thank you very much, sir. Come again." Anyway, I'd had fun rolling the phrases around on the back of my tongue and trying to sound nasal.

I walked to Saint-Germain, stopped for a drink at the Caféaux Deux Magots and imagined Appollinaire scribbling on a napkin, "In the end you are tired of this ancient world," imagined his lassitude in the geography of Paris before the wars when Orly was a novelty. I longed for another time. I lingered by a shop on the Rue de Rivoli and contemplated buying a black velvet suit, a perfect cloak of emancipation, but I had no energy for fittings. The very act of shopping could always destroy my cupidity. I had eggs Benedict for lunch in the tearoom above an English-language bookstore and played eye games with a girl across the room. Maybe she wanted to know me. But I couldn't introduce myself to strange women, at least not when I was sober. I walked past my hotel and through the Place Vendôme, past the Ritz. My mother had always wanted my father to take her to Paris and to stay at the Ritz. Maybe now she'd come alone. I turned down the Rue de la Paix and saw a small brown sign overhanging the sidewalk: "Harry's New York Bar," where the concierge had said it would be. The bar was empty. I had a gin-and-tonic and talked with the bartender about the White Sox's chances for the pennant, though I knew very little about baseball. I looked at the faded pennants around the cornice and found the familiar green and white of Michigan State University. I would have preferred that it hadn't been there. I looked at the photos jammed together on the walls and found one of Hemingway wearing a tweed sports coat and holding a large trout in his arms as if he was showing off a baby.

It had gotten cloudy, and I walked in the Tuileries. I followed a beautiful dark-haired woman in a maxi-coat. I knew there was no chance of our meeting. She probably didn't speak English, but I followed her. She walked as if she were killing time, her hands in the pockets of her coat, swinging one leg forward and then the other. I lingered so as not to overtake her. She descended the steps to an underground toilet, and I walked on. I saw a group of children gathered around a Punch and Judy show and stopped to watch. Near the edge of the park, some boys were kicking a soccer ball.

I sat on a bench and looked at the new leaves and at the flowers. I think some of them were anemones, daughters of the wind. Mary Lou had told me she liked anemones. I fell asleep on the bench. When I woke up it was almost evening. It took me a moment to remember where I was, and I rubbed my eyes to clear them. I looked at the ground between my feet, and then at my shoes, the walking shoes I'd bought in Detroit the day after I left home. They were a bit scarred and scuffed, but the stitching was sound. I thought of all the places I'd worn the shoes, all the people I'd been with since I bought them. Things had been so simple before I bought these shoes, dull but simple. It had passed for happiness, whatever it was. "I've had a lot of unhappiness wearing these shoes. It's not the shoes' fault, of course." I began to feel slightly stoned, not really high, but just as if I were beginning to come out of myself. I felt my pockets and found my airline ticket folder. I propped it on my knee and began to write.

I've had a lot of unhappiness
wearing these shoes
It's not the shoes' fault, of course
I decided to mess up my life
and wearing these shoes walked out
Now the shoes won't let me
love what I love anymore
They force me to move
I'm constantly lachrymose
and stain them with tears
They hiss at my slippers
trembling in the closet
They're ruining my sleep my peace of mind
but honestly they're comfortable
and they look like the man
I've always wanted to be

One day they'll wear out
though I polish them often
The stitching will fray
my toes protrude through the uppers
Things will be better

I'll buy shoes made on a different last
perhaps without soles.

Another poem, perhaps it was a poem. I folded the ticket folder, put it in my coat pocket and walked back to the hotel.

29

The whole thing was insane. I spent hours tiptoeing between Gloria's room and Mary Lou's, assuaging damaged pride. It was like trying to patch a leaky dam with bubble gum, the wall flexing and bulging with the force of the flood. Gloria greeted me like a mistral. Her chin seemed to protrude more than I had remembered. She demanded contrition and a servile return to Brainard, where I might attempt, during the rest of my life, to mollify the embarrassment and disgrace I'd caused the family. "Gee, I'm sorry," I was to say again and again to everyone I met. I didn't use that word "Gee" anymore. I told her about Mary Lou and that she, too, was in Paris. The atmosphere became tense.

"You what?"

"I want you to meet her."

"This time you're really going too far."

"What does that mean?"

"It means I thought you wanted a reconciliation, not a reconstruction of your sordid little interlude."

"Reconciliation on whose terms?"

"On my terms. I am your wife. I do have certain rights in this matter."

"What have rights got to do with it?"

"Rights are what's right. That's what."

"I don't give a damn about what's right. I just want to know what is."

We seemed to have taken up right where we were before I'd left home, except now Gloria had her damaged rights to be indignant about. I tried to imagine what it would be like to go back to Brainard with her, but the only image was that of a television screen doing flop-overs.

We had dinner together at a little restaurant on the Rue Marbuef. She wanted to go to Maxim's but I refused. We ate in a cool silence, broken only over dessert when she told me the most recent Brainard scandal: Raymond Travis and his wife had been kicked out of the Goosepoint Country Club for failure to pay their dues.

"What are you telling me that for? I don't give a damn about that."

"I just thought you'd be interested. You never did like Ray Travis, and his wife's such a climber. Everyone at the club thinks so."

"Jesus H. Christ. I've been gone for three months, lived in a whole new world, and you come all the way to Paris to tell me Sally Travis is a social climber. I don't give a damn if Sally Travis is a social climber. I don't give a damn if she's a tree climber. She's free to climb anything or anyone she wants to."

"Well, don't think it hasn't happened."

"What hasn't happened?"

"Don't think Sally Travis hasn't been getting around."

"Goddamn it, Gloria, you just don't understand. I hope she does get around. I hope everyone gets around. Do you mean she's fucking other men? Is that what you're trying to say?"

"Oh, Larry, don't be crude."

"Oh, now I'm being crude because I take the veneer off the garbage you're trying to tell me? That's very interesting. I guess I must be a little warped to use language like that. My, my, whatever has happened to me head. Tch, tch, tch, tch, tch," I said, lapsing into Bugs Bunny. "What a ba-a-a-d boy. Oh, if my mommy could only hear me now."

"Your mommy would be appalled," she said.

"I don't think you know my mommy very well. She doesn't appall. And speaking of my mother, you might have told me how she is. You might have told me about the children."

"I didn't think you'd be interested."

"No, no, of course not. Perverse little me. What I really want to know is who has Sally Travis been screwing."

"Larry, you're disgusting."

"I've got something to say to you, Gloria."

"Yes?"

"Sally Travis takes it in the ass."

"Stop it, Larry."

"No, it's true. All the boys at the club say it's true."

"I want to go back to the hotel." She spit the words out through clenched teeth. "Take me back to the hotel this instant."

"Yes, dear," I said, calling for the check.

Mary Lou was sweet. We didn't have a lot to talk about, but conversation was never her long suit. She was sorry she had left me in Hermosa Beach. "I should have known you'd come back," she said.

"It wasn't your fault," I said. "I was acting like an asshole." I told her about the red-eyed man I found in our motel room when I went back, and she started to laugh.

"It wasn't funny at the time," I said.

"I know, poor baby. I've thought about you a lot since then. I even went back to Benton Harbor. I knew it was the only place you might look for me."

I started to tell her about the transvestite I'd almost fallen in love with, but she put her arms around my neck and kissed me just below the ear. I wanted to tell her about Mona and Georgette. I wanted to tell her about everything, but I felt myself sinking to the bed, pulling her with me. Her hands slid under my shirt, and her fingers played over my chest. One hand fumbled with my belt buckle. I reached down to help her. "We shouldn't be doing this now," I said. I felt for the zipper at the back of her dress.

I could never find Kalab. While I was occupied with Gloria and Mary Lou, he was either drunk, stoned, or lost. Twice he called the hotel, and I had to go to Montmartre to pick him up. He was more a burden than an aide-de-camp. His headband was cocked and sat high on his head. He looked like a drunken Jesus.

"Larry, my pants hurt. I saw a woman down there in Pig Alley, and she made my pants hurt." I was trying to get him into the shower. "It's a fantastic idea," he said. "A fantastic idea to get us all together. I'm glad to be here to help you, Larry." He'd been arrested for trying to sell his clothes on the street in the Place Pigalle. He'd apparently sold his shoes and shirt, because all he had when I brought him back to the hotel were his Levis, his sports coat, and his necktie, which was green and looked absurd against his bare chest.

I had carefully arranged a dinner party in the hotel restaurant, a table in the corner, soft lights, an ample supply of chilled Chablis, and I wanted to be sure Kalab would be there. He was to be a buffer. As the natural center of attention, he might absorb some of the scrutiny of two faced-off females, act as a foil, the sullen ground on which base metal might glitter. "I'm going to help you, Larry," he said, as I turned on the water, "We're going to straighten out your life." By five the detumescence of his skull was almost complete.

Mary Lou was already seated at the table when I arrived. I kissed her on the cheek and took the seat next to her. She was drinking a whisky sour on the rocks and I ordered a gin-and-tonic. We sat silently for what seemed a long time.

"The cut flowers are lovely," she said.

"Yes, they are."

"This sure isn't like back home."

There was another long silence. We finished our drinks and ordered two more. I saw Gloria in the lobby, and my stomach began to flutter. I stood up and waved to her. The maître d' escorted her to the table and seated her with an unctuous flourish. She'd wasted no time in discovering the splendors of Paris. She was elegant in her coiffure and new silk dress.

"Gloria, this is Mary Lou."

Gloria smiled with her lips only and then fixed her vision somewhere just above Mary Lou's head. Mary Lou stared at her drink.

"May I order you a drink, Gloria?"

"Oh, that would be nice," she said, smiling too broadly and sneaking a perusal of Mary Lou. "I'll have a Bloody Mary, if you don't mind." I choked on my own saliva and began coughing.

"Are you all right?" Mary Lou asked.

"I haven't any idea," I said, still coughing.

I motioned to the waiter and ordered a vodka and tomato juice. There was another long silence. Gloria looked at me and then at Mary Lou. "Well, isn't this jolly?" she said. I tried to take another sip of my gin-and-tonic, but it seemed to freeze in the glass and I couldn't get it past my lips.

Kalab arrived wearing cowboy boots and a blue serge suit that vibrated against his red moustache and ponytail. He wore a large gold ring in his left ear. He kissed Mary Lou on the cheek. He turned to Gloria, took her hand and kissed it. "*Enchanté, madame.* Your reputation is exceeded only by your great beauty and animal magnetism."

"Oh, cut the crap," Gloria said.

"Thank you," Tom said. "I needed that."

"This is Tom Kalab."

"Really? I thought it was Charles Boyer."

Tom began to roll a Bull Durham cigarette and ordered a double bourbon-and-water. He spilled some tobacco on the tablecloth and blew it away. A few flakes landed in the lap of Gloria's new silk dress.

"Well," he said, "I suggest we begin with an appropriate toast, but I haven't got the vaguest notion of what that might be." He emptied his glass and ordered another. "Well, Larry, where shall we begin?"

"With hors d'oeuvres," I suggested.

The maitre d' hovered like a bird of prey. Tom turned to him. "Hors d'oeuvres, garcon, s'il vous plaît." His French was totally without accent.

I felt the floor beginning to open beneath my chair. I began to realize I was a coward, not the kind of coward who would avoid danger altogether, but a worse kind of coward who would court it to the brink with bravado and then back away at the crucial moment, like the matador who would dedicate the last bull of his career to the crowd, the president, his wife, his mistress, the Holy Mother, and the memory of Manolete, then ask his assistant to kill it because he didn't like the way it was looking at him. I had planned a showdown, courted resolution, and now I was afraid of it. I wanted the evening to be devoted to pleasantries. We could enjoy dinner and drinks, tell a few good stories, brandy off, and all go happily to bed glowing with companionship and good will.

"The cut flowers are beautiful," I said. Tom and Gloria looked at me as if I'd announced I was going to fart.

"The cut flowers?" Tom said.

"Yes. Mary Lou and I were commenting on them just before you came."

"Really?" Tom said.

"What else did you comment on?" Gloria asked. She put a particular emphasis on the word "comment."

"Oh, just on the flowers and the fact that things in Paris are very different from the way they are back home."

"I'm just beginning to realize how different they are," Tom said. "You know, Larry, you're really a very perceptive dude."

Mary Lou looked at me. She didn't know what to say. The waiter came with a tray of caviar, onions, egg, lemon, and wafers. For a moment I imagined myself on the table, a sprig of parsley on my upper lip. Three condors bowed their heads and clacked their talons, waiting for the leader to take the first bite. They were waiting for me while I tried to prove I could cross the Sahara. They didn't seem to be in any hurry. They knew time was on their side. There's nothing you can prove to a condor.

Tom dipped into the caviar. The waiter brought more drinks. Tom was the king condor and took the first bite.

"Well, where shall we begin the negotiations?" he asked. He winked at me. It was the wink of the hangman.

"Negotiations?" Gloria said, craning her neck and wiping her beak on her wing feathers.

"Yes," Tom said. "The negotiations for Larry." I saw a chart on the wall, a sectional diagram of my body, describing the use of each part: chuck roast, butt steak, short ribs, tenderloin.

"Whatever are you talking about?" Gloria squawked. I heard the screech of tires, and the room felt slightly unstable.

"I mean what are you willing to put up for him?" Now I could smell burning rubber and the sickly sweet smell of castor oil.

"You must be kidding." A light tap on my rear fender, and a white car filled my rear-view mirrors. Mary Lou looked at me. I was watching the concrete wall sail into my windshield.

"I'm taking bids," Tom said. "Now, what are you willing to put up for him?" He leaned toward Gloria and squinted like an auctioneer.

"This is what I'm willing to put up for him," Gloria said, raising her right hand and extending the middle finger in front of Tom's nose.

The air was full of fire and flying debris. I saw the frightened spectators trying to flee. They'd come too close for a look at the gore. The car exploded, and now they were trying to get away. One man had his arms full of hot dogs. I started to laugh.

"Very well," Tom said. "I have the first bid." He turned to Mary Lou. "Now what are you willing to bid, my dear?" Mary Lou began laughing. "Ah your teeth, your beautiful white teeth," he said, turning back to Gloria.

The waiter came with fire extinguisher and tried to put out the laughter.

"It's a standoff, Larry," Tom said, "a Mexican standoff. This can only be resolved in a trial by combat." The waiter was pouring wine. "A sexual tournament to

see who can perform the most outrageous fandangos."
The room was filled with sirens and laughter.

"I'll be the judge and the consolation prize, so whoever loses, loses you, but doesn't lose much, if you see what I mean. Ha, ha, ha." His laughter began slowly and accelerated to an almost hysterical cackle. He was trying to drink at the same time, choking on his wine and spattering the tablecloth with purple spots as if he were spitting starch and preparing to iron it. Two waiters came and helped him to the men's room. All I could see through the fire and smoke were Mary Lou's beautiful teeth and the cords of her neck straining with laughter.

Gloria was gone.

We went for a walk along the Tuileries. The air seemed very cool. "It's a mistake to try to resolve these things," I said. "They have a way of resolving themselves." I told her I was leaving in the morning. I told her I'd try to call her in a week or so. She said she'd like that. I saw my life rushing into a funnel. I was happy. I told her it was the way she laughed. I loved the way she laughed.

I've read that the polar ice cap is melting and that soon it will begin snowing in the Arctic, more snow than a summer can melt. As the snow builds, the sheer weight will force it to break loose and begin moving toward the equator. Year by year we will watch it grow thicker and move down on us. Not even Paris will be spared. We will watch it scraped clean, like the stacks of chips from a faro table, by a shelf of ice two miles high. In fifty million years the sun will flare up and scorch the earth clean. Nothing will be left.

I would return to Paris, I promised myself, perhaps to stay. I sat up in bed and turned on the light. I ripped a page from my *French Phrase Book* and wrote the promise out, a note that must be paid. I folded the page, slipped it between the cards in my wallet and turned out the light.

I was falling down a long black tube, scratching at the walls as I fell. Each scratch became a patch of light, and I could see how far I'd fallen by the patches of light above me. All was black below me as I fell, but I began to imagine the patches I would make farther down the tube. My life became defined in those little patches of light as I touched the wall and let go, each patch growing smaller as I fell until the farthest ones became like stars. They never grew smaller than that. I saw a remote lake in British Columbia where I lived in a small log cabin. Though fishing had been a velleity, I saw myself standing in the bow of a long, flat-bottomed boat. A hundred feet of white fly line looped, then straightened behind me. It contrasted brilliantly with the dark evergreens that bordered the lake. I was fishing for food. A woman moved about in the cabin. I knew it was a woman by the way she moved. I couldn't see her face, but I knew I loved her. The vision of the lake became a patch of light, glowing against the wall of the endless tube, and grew smaller as I fell away from it. I tried to scratch another vision like it. I kept on trying, but it never came clear. The lake had now become a star, brighter than the others, and I heard Mary Lou laughing. She reached up with her lips, cocking her head as if she were trying to kiss me. I touched the wall and scratched off another patch of light. Each patch was a new beginning. I stared at the light of the lake star. It grew small and sane swimming into my head. I could no longer feel myself falling.

30

It had turned cold when I got to Brainard. Though it was the first week in June, it seemed more like April. The sky was gray, and the temperature hung in the mid-forties. I rented a car at the airport and drove to my mother's house. I'd considered visiting the children first, but I had a vague idea they might be frightened of me. Perhaps they wouldn't even recognize me. A new maid answered the door. I told her I was Mrs. Bancroft's son and asked if I might see her. The maid said, "Just a minute." She didn't look as if she believed me. She closed the door and I was left standing in the cold wind staring at the dark mahogany door and the brass knocker engraved with the name of Bancroft, the door I'd entered freely as a child. I thought how many times I'd dreaded that innocuous door as a prelude to another subtly vicious family fête. I turned and looked at the Russian olive trees in the yard, the wind blowing through their silver leaves, how they seemed more silver in the cold and wind. They'd been planted when I was fifteen. I'm sure they'd grown a great deal since then, but I couldn't really remember how small they'd been. I considered devising a story of spurious noble encounters in the months I'd been gone, of having found and redeemed myself through travels among and altruistic acts toward the world's unfortunate, but dismissed the thought. Soon the maid came back to the door. "I'm sorry for making you stand out there," she said. "Mrs. Bancroft will see you. You're to go upstairs."

I'd always considered my mother an adjunct to my father and was surprised to see how much her own, how distinct and separate she now appeared. She met me at the door to her sitting room, stopped for a moment, and looked at me. Then she came to me and hugged me, the top of her head resting just below my chin. She was all perfume and powder, and I remembered how I'd longed for that smell when I was a child away at school. I laughed to myself at my notion of impressing her as we embraced. She was sniffling slightly, and she hugged me for a long time. Then she looked up and kissed me. She moved back at arms' length and looked at me.

"You're thinner," she said. "Maybe it's just that your hair's longer, but no, you are thinner. I can see it in your cheeks."

She took me by the arm and led me into the room. I sat down. She sat across from me and looked at me for a long time.

"Would you like something to eat?"

"No, thanks. I ate on the plane."

"Some coffee?"

"No, thanks."

There was another pause. "It didn't go well with Gloria in Paris?" she asked, then added, "No, of course it didn't. I knew that. Gloria went to Paris trying to prove something, and there wasn't anything to prove."

Her head seemed to nod involuntarily, and she turned and gazed out the window. It seemed a long time before she spoke. "We had some bluebirds this spring. All the plantings finally paid off. Your father would have enjoyed them, would have enjoyed knowing we'd finally enticed them to come, would have enjoyed knowing that even more." Her voice trailed off and she said something else I couldn't hear, still looking out the window. She smiled and dabbed around her eyes with her handkerchief. "Well, Larry, what are you going to do?" she asked, then quickly, "No, I don't expect an answer. That doesn't matter right now."

"I feel I should say something," I said, half laughing, "but I don't know what it is."

"I know," she said.